"THIS IS YOUR OWN DO-IT-YOURSELF DEATH KIT."

"The *new* guaranteed Murder Kit, with the double-your-money-back warranty, for your protection."

Well, she thought, frugally, that's nice, anyway. *That double-your-money-back thing.*

"This Kit contains three sure, clean and unde-tectable, I repeat, *undetectable,* ways to com-mit murder. No two kits are the same. Each of the three *modus operandi* is designed for you according to the application blank you sent us when you contracted for this Kit. Now. To prepare yourself for your murder—"

She snapped the pamphlet shut with quick, suddenly sweating hands. *Do I hate him that much? Yes, yes, I hate him that much and more!*

She opened the pamphlet again.

"The first method of murder we have prepared for you. . . ."

—from "Do-It-Yourself"

Other SIGNET Science Fiction You'll Enjoy

ELLISON WONDERLAND

Harlan Ellison

A SIGNET BOOK

NEW AMERICAN LIBRARY

TIMES MIRROR

Copyright © 1962, 1974 by Harlan Ellison

All rights reserved. No part of this book may be reproduced in any form without permission in writing from the Author or the Author's Agent, except by a reviewer who may quote brief passages in a review to be printed in a magazine or newspaper, or electronically transmitted on radio or television.
For information address Author's Agent: Robert P. Mills, Ltd., 156 East 52nd Street, New York, New York 10022.

ACKNOWLEDGMENTS

"Commuter's Problem" and "In Lonely Lands" appeared in *Fantastic Universe*, copyright, 1957, 1958, by King-Size Publications, Inc. "The Very Last Day of a Good Woman" (under the title "The Last Day"), "Deal from the Bottom" and "Do-It-Yourself" (written with Joe L. Hensley) appeared in *Rogue Magazine*, copyright, 1958, 1960, 1961, by Greenleaf Publishing Company. "The Silver Corridor" appeared in *Infinity Science Fiction*, copyright, 1956, by Royal Publications, Inc. "Gnomebody," and "The Wind Beyond the Mountains" (under the title "Savage Wind") appeared in *Amazing Stories*, copyright, 1956, 1958, by Ziff-Davis Publishing Company. "Back to the Drawing Boards" appeared in *Fantastic Universe*, copyright, 1958, by King-Size Publications, Inc. "The Sky Is Burning" appeared in *If: Worlds of Science Fiction*, copyright, 1958, by Quinn Publishing Company, Inc. "Mealtime" (under the title "A Case of Ptomaine") and "Battlefield" (under the title "His First Day at War") appeared in *Space Travel Magazine*, copyright, 1958, by Greenleaf Publishing Company. "Nothing for my Noon Meal" appeared in *Nebula Science Fiction*, copyright, 1958, by Peter Hamilton, Limited (Scotland). "Hadj" appeared in *Science Fiction Adventures*, copyright, 1956, by Royal Publications, Inc. and subsequently reprinted in the *New York Post Weekend Magazine* for October 28, 1956. "Rain, Rain, Go Away" appeared in *Science-Fantasy Magazine*, copyright, 1956, by Nova Publications, Limited (England). "All the Sounds of Fear" appeared in the *Saint Detective Magazine* (French and English editions), copyright, 1962, by Fiction Publishing Company.

Published by arrangement with the Author and the Author's Agent, Robert P. Mills, Ltd.

SIGNET, SIGNET CLASSICS, MENTOR, PLUME and MERIDIAN BOOKS
are published by The New American Library, Inc.,
1301 Avenue of the Americas, New York, New York 10019

First Printing, August, 1974

1 2 3 4 5 6 7 8 9

PRINTED IN THE UNITED STATES OF AMERICA

The original edition bore this dedication:

This random group of leftover dreams and wry conspiracies I offer to Wednesday's Child . . .

KENNY

with love and pride, and more than just a touch of sorrow.

Fourteen years later, and links of the broken chain have been joined once more, not welded shut, but merely joined. And so, with fourteen years' more love and pride, and with that touch of sorrow removed, once again I offer this ragbag of illusions to His Own Man . . .

KENNY

Contents

ELLISON
WONDERLAND

Introduction
The Man On The Mushroom

The arrival in Hollywood was something less than auspicious. It was February, 1962, and I had broken free of the human monster for whom I'd been editing in Chicago. It was one of the worst times in my life. The one time I'd ever felt the need to go to a psychiatrist, that time in Chicago. I had remarried in haste after the four-year anguish of Charlotte and the Army and the hand-to-mouth days in Greenwich Village; now I was living to repent in agonizing leisure.

I had been crazed for two years and hadn't realized it. Now I was responsible for one of the nicest women in the world, and her son, a winner by *any* standards, and I found I had messed their lives by entwining them with mine. There was need for me to run, but I could not. Nice Jewish boys from Ohio don't cut and abandon. So I began doing berserk things. I committed personal acts of a demeaning and reprehensible nature, involved myself in liaisons that were doomed and purposeless, went steadily more insane as the days wound tighter than a mainspring.

Part of it was money. Not really, but I thought it was the major part of the solution to the situation. And I'd banked on selling a book of stories to the very man for whom I was working. He took considerable pleasure in waiting till we were at a business lunch, with several other people, to announce he was not buying the book. (The depth of his sadism is obvious when one learns he subsequently *did* buy and publish the book.)

But at that moment, it was as though someone had split the earth under me and left me hanging by the ragged edge, by my fingertips. I went back to the tiny, empty office he had set up in a downtown Evanston office building, and I sat at my desk staring at the wall. There

1

was a clock on the wall in front of me. When I sat down after that terrible lunch, it was 1:00. . . .

When I looked at the clock a moment later, it was 3:15. . . .

The next time I looked, a moment later, it was 4:45. . . .
Then 5:45 . . .
Then 6:15 . . .
7:00 . . . 8:30 . . .

Somehow, I don't know how, even today, I laid my head on the desk, and when I opened my eyes again I had taken the phone off the hook. It was lying beside my mouth. A long time later, and again I don't remember doing it, I dialed a friend, Frank M. Robinson, a dear writer friend of many years.

I heard Frank's voice saying, "Hello . . . hello . . . is someone there . . . ?"

"Frank . . . help me . . ."

And when my head was lifted off the desk, it was an hour later, the phone was whistling with a disconnect tone, and Frank had made it all the way across from Chicago to Evanston to find me. He held me like a child, and I cried.

Soon after, I left Evanston and Chicago and the human monster, and with my wife and her son began the long trek to the West Coast. We had agreed to divorce, but she had said to me, with a very special wisdom that I never perceived till much later, when I was whole again, "As long as you're going to leave me, at least take me to where it's warm."

But we had no money. So we had to go to Los Angeles by way of New York from Chicago. If I could sell a book, I would have the means to go West, young man, go West. (And *that* was the core of the problem, not money: I was a *young* man. I was twenty-eight, but I had never become an adult.)

In a broken-down 1957 Ford we limped across to New York during the worst snowstorms in thirty years. My wife and her son stayed with a friend I'd known in the Village, and I slept on the sofa at the home of Leo & Diane Dillon, the two finest artists I know. Leo & Diane slept on the floor. They are more than merely friends.

It was December of 1961, and amid the tensions and horrors of that eight-week stay in New York, two things happened that brought momentary light, and helped me keep hold:

The first was a review by Dorothy Parker in *Esquire* of a small-printing paperback collection of my stories. How she had obtained it I do not know. (When I met her, later, in Hollywood, she was unable to remember where the book had come from.) But she raved about it, and said I had talent, and it was the first really substantial affirmative notice from a major critic. It altered the course of my writing career, and provided my ego—which had been nourishing itself cannibalistically on itself—with reason for feeling I could write.

The second happening of light was the sale of this book. Gerry Gross bought it for short money, mostly because he knew I was in a bad way. But it provided the funds to start out for Los Angeles.

We traveled a hard road down through the Southwest, and in Fort Worth we were staved in by a drunken cowboy in a pickup. Rear-ended. He had a carhop on one arm, and a fifth of Teacher's in the free hand. Rammed us on an icy bridge, smashed the car, crushed the rear-end trunk containing our luggage and my typewriter, and I suppose it was that typewriter that saved our lives. The typewriter has paid the rent and put food on the table many times, but that time it physically gave up its life to save me.

We were laid up in Fort Worth for a week, with our money running out. Had it not been for the help of the then-police chief, a man whose name I'll never forget— Cato Hightower—we would never have gotten out of Texas. He got me a new typewriter, had the car repaired for a fraction of what the garage would have stiffed a tourist just passing through and he paid off the motel.

I arrived in Los Angeles in January of 1962 with exactly ten cents in my pocket. For the last three hundred miles we had not eaten. There wasn't enough money for gas *and* food. All we'd had to keep us alive was a box of pecan pralines we'd bought before the accident and had in the rear seat.

The arrival in Hollywood was something less than auspicious.

My almost-ex-wife and her son moved into an apartment, and I took up residence in a fourteen-dollar-a-week room in a bungalow complex that is now an empty lot on Wilshire Boulevard. I tried to get work in television, got some assignments that paid the various rents, and bombed out on all of them. Nobody had bothered to show me how to write a script. And when it looked as though I'd hit the very bottom, ELLISON WONDERLAND was published in June of 1962, the publisher sent me a copy, and the check for the balance of monies due on publication. It was enough to pull me through till I got another assignment—writing *Burke's Law* for the Four Star Studios and ABC. It was the very moment my luck changed.

I remember the morning the mail arrived, with the book in its little manila envelope. I ripped open the package, and out fell the check. But I didn't even look at it. I sat in that room smelling of mildew and stared at the cover of *Ellison Wonderland*. The artist, Sandy Kossin, had taken a photo of me, and he'd drawn me in sitting cross-legged atop a giant mushroom, while all around me danced and capered the characters from the stories in this book. Skidoop and Ithk and Helgorth Labbula and the crocodile-headed woman from "The Silver Corridor" and that little jazzbo gnome with the patois now long-outdated and *so* unhip.

There I was. And Hollywood became, for the first time since I'd arrived, not a grungy, lonely, frustrating town whose tinsel could strangle you . . . but a magic town whose sidewalks *were* paved with gold; a yellow brick road leading to a giant mushroom where I could perch if I simply hung in there.

Now it's fourteen years later, and ELLISON WONDERLAND is back in print, thanks to the good offices of Michael Seidman and Olga Vezeris of New American Library.

And just to show that fairy tales sometimes *do* have happy endings, dear readers be advised I'm really okay now. There *is* a mushroom, and I'm sitting on it, and I've been writing better here in magic town than I ever did anywhere else, and I'll keep on doing it till I run out of mushroom or magic (and that is *not* a reference to dope, which I don't, so I ain't), and here, like a good penny, is ELLISON WONDERLAND again.

Welcome to *my* world.

HARLAN ELLISON

Los Angeles
March, 1974

The trouble with Miniver Cheevy (child of scorn who cursed the day that he was born) was that—aside from the fact he was a bit of a fink, with no understanding of the contemporary image he projected—he was always building dream castles, and then trying to move into them. It's muddy thinking, youth, to expect to do any better in another epoch than the one you're in. A guy who is a foul ball in one time, must assuredly be so in another . . . unless his name is da Vinci or Hieronymous Bosch. And the poor soul in this little epic is named neither, which may be the reason he suffers a

commuter's problem

"Thing" was all I could call it, and it had a million tentacles.

It was growing in Da Campo's garden, and it kept *staring* at me.

"How's *your* garden, John," said Da Campo behind me, and I spun, afraid he'd see my face was chalk-white and terrified.

"Oh—pretty, pretty good. I was just looking for Jamie's baseball. It rolled in here." I tried to laugh gaily, but it got stuck on my pylorus. "Afraid the lad's getting too strong an arm for his old man. Can't keep up these days."

I pretended to be looking for the ball, trying not to catch Da Campo's eyes. They were steel-grey and disturbing. He pointed to the hardball in my hand, "That it?"

"Huh? Oh, yeah, yeah! I was just going back to the boy. Well, take it easy. I'll—uh—I'll see you—uh—at the Civic Center, won't I?"

"You suspect, don't you, John?"

"Suspect? Uh—suspect? Suspect what?"

I didn't wait to let him clarify the comment. I'm afraid I left hurriedly. I crushed some of his rhododendrons.

When I got back to my own front yard I did something I've never had occasion to do before. I mopped my

7

brow with my handkerchief. The good monogrammed hankie from my lapel pocket, not the all-purpose one in my hip pocket; the one I use on my glasses. That shows you how unnerved I was.

The hankie came away wet.

"Hey, Dad!"

I jumped four feet, but by the time I came down I realized it was my son, Jamie, not Clark Da Campo coming after me. "Here, Jamie, go on over to the schoolyard and shag a few with the other kids. I have to do some work in the house."

I tossed him the ball and went up the front steps. Charlotte was running one of those hideous claw-like attachments over the drapes, and the vacuum cleaner was howling at itself. I had a vague urge to run out of the house and go into the woods somewhere to hide—where there weren't any drapes, or vacuum cleaners, or staring tentacled plants.

"I'm going into the den. I don't want to be disturbed for about two hours, Char—" She didn't turn.

I stepped over and kicked the switch on the floor unit. The howling died off and she smiled at me over her shoulder, "Now you're a saboteur?"

I couldn't help chuckling, even worried as I was; Charlotte's like that. "Look, Poison, I've got some deep thought to slosh around in for a while. Make sure the kid and the bill collectors don't get to me, will you."

She nodded, and added as an afterthought, "Still have to go into the city today?"

"Umm. 'Fraid so. There's something burning in the Gillings Mills account and they dumped the whole brief on my desk."

She made a face that said, "Another Saturday shot," and shrugged.

I gave her a rush-kiss and went into the den, closing and locking the big double doors behind me.

Symmetry and order are tools for me, so I decided to put down on paper my assets and liabilities in this matter. Or, more accurately, just what I was sure of, and what I wasn't.

In the asset column went things like:

Name: John Weiler. I work for a trade association. In

this case the trade association is made up of paper manufacturers. I'm a commuter—a man in the grey flannel suit, if you would. A family man. One wife, Charlotte; one son, Jamie; one vacuum cleaner, noisy.

I own my own home, I have a car and enough money to go up to Grossingers once each Summer mainly on the prodding of Charlotte, who feels I should broaden myself more. We keep up with the Joneses, without too much trouble.

I do my job well, I'm a climbing executive type and I'm well-adjustedly happy. I'm a steady sort of fellow and I keep my nose out of other people's business primarily because I have enough small ones of my own. I vote regularly, not just talk about it, and I gab a lot with my fellow suburbanites about our gardens—sort of a universal hobby in the sticks.

Forty-seven minutes into town on the train five days a week (and sometimes Saturday, which was happening all too frequently lately) and Lexington Avenue greets me. My health and the family's is good, except for an occasional twinge in my stomach, so most of the agony in the world stays away from me. I don't get worried easily, because I stay out of other people's closets.

But this time I was worried worse than just badly.

I drew a line and started writing in the liabilities column:

Item: Clark Da Campo has a million-tentacled staring plant in his garden that is definitely *not* of normal botanical origin.

Item: There has never been a wisp of smoke from the Da Campo chimney, even during the coldest days of the Winter.

Item: Though they have been living here for six months, the Da Campos have never made a social call, attended a local function, shown up at a public place.

Item: Charlotte has told me she has never seen Mrs. Da Campo buy any groceries or return any empty bottles or hang out any wash.

Item: There are no lights in the Da Campo household after six o'clock every night, and full-length drapes are drawn at the same time.

Item: I am scared witless.

Then I looked at the sheet. There was a great deal more

on the asset side than the other, but somehow, after all
the value I'd placed on the entries in that first column,
those in the second had suddenly become more impressive, overpowering, alarming. And they were so nebulous,
so inconclusive, I didn't know what it was about them
that scared me.

But it looked like I was in Da Campo's closets whether
I wanted to be or not.

Three hours later the house had assumed the dead
sogginess of a quiet Saturday afternoon, three pages of
note-paper were covered with obscure but vaguely omi-
nous doodles, and I was no nearer an answer that made
sense than when I'd gone into the den.

I sighed and threw down my pencil.

My back was stiff from sitting at the desk, and I got
up to find the pain multiplied along every inch of my
spinal cord. I slid the asset-liability evaluation under my
blotter and cleaned the cigarette ashes off the desk where
I'd missed the ashtray.

Then I dumped the ashtray in the waste basket. It
was Saturday and Charlotte frowned on dirty ashtrays left
about, even in my private territory.

When I came out the place was still as a tomb, and I
imagined Charlotte had gone into the downtown section
of our hamlet to gawk at the exclusive shops and their
exclusive contents.

I went into the kitchen and looked through the window. The car was gone, bearing out my suspicions. My
eyes turned themselves heavenward and my mind reeled
out bank balances without prompting.

"Want to talk now, John?"

I could have sworn my legs were made of ice and they
were melting me down to the kitchen linoleum. I turned
around and—that's right—Da Campo was in the doorway
to the dining room.

"What do you want?" I bluffed, stepping forward
threateningly.

"I came over to borrow a cup of sugar and talk a
little, John," said Da Campo, smiling.

The utter incongruity of it! Borrowing a cup of sugar!
It was too funny to equate with weird plants and odd

goings-on in the house across the street. It took the edge off my belligerence quite effectively.

"S-sure, I suppose I can find the wife's sugar." Then it occurred to me: "How do you know my name?"

"How do you know mine?"

"Why I—I asked the neighbors. Like to know who's living across the street, that's all."

"Well, that's how I know yours, John. I asked my neighbors."

"Which ones? The Schwachters? Heffman? Brown?"

He waved his hand absently, "Oh . . . just the neighbors, that's all. How about that sugar?"

I opened one of the cabinets and took out the sugar bowl. Da Campo didn't have a cup, so I took one down—one of the old blue set—and filled it for him.

"Thanks," he said, "feel like that talk now?"

Somehow, I wasn't frightened of him, as I was by that sheet of items. It was easy to feel friendly toward the big, grey-eyed, grey-haired man in the sport shirt and slacks. Just another typical suburban neighbor.

"Sure, come on into the living room," I answered, moving past him.

When Da Campo had found a reasonably comfortable position in one of Charlotte's doubly-damned modern chairs, I tried to make small conversation. "I've never noticed a TV antenna on your house. Don't tell me an inside one works over there. No one this far out seems to be able to make one of those gadgets bring in anything decently."

"We don't have television."

"Oh," I said.

The silence hauled itself around the room several times, and I tried again. "Uh—how come we never see you at the new Civic Center? Got some sweet bowling alleys down there and the little theatre group is pretty decent. Like to see—"

"Look, John, I thought I might come over and try to explain about myself, about us—Ellie and me." He seemed so intent, so earnest, I leaned forward.

"What do you mean? You don't have to—"

"No, no, I mean it," he cut me off. "I know everyone in the neighborhood has been wondering about us. Why we don't go out much, why we don't invite you over, everything like that." He held up his hands in fumbling motions, as though he were looking for the words. Then he let his hands fall, as though he knew he would never find the words.

"No, I don't think anyone has—"

He stopped me again with a shake of the head. His eyes were very deep and very sad and I didn't quite know what to say. I suddenly realized how far out of touch with real people I'd gotten in my years of commuting. There's something cold and impersonal about a nine-to-five job and a ride home with total strangers. Even total strangers that live in the same town. I just looked at Da Campo.

"It's simple, really," he said, rubbing his hands together, looking down at them as though they had just grown from the ends of his arms.

"I got mixed up with some pretty strange people a few years ago, and well, I went to jail for a while. When I came out I couldn't get a job and we had to move. By then Ellie had drawn into a shell and . . . well, it just hasn't been easy."

I didn't know why he was telling me all this and I found myself embarrassed. I looked around for something to break the tension, and then pulled out a pack of cigarettes. I held them out to him and he looked up from his hands for a second, shaking his head. He went back to staring at them as I lit a cigarette. I was hoping he wouldn't go on, but he did.

"Reason I'm telling you this is that you must have thought me pretty odd this afternoon. The only thing I have is my garden, and Ellie, and we don't like living as alone as we do, but it's better this way. That's the way we have to do it. At least for a while."

For a second I got the impression he had skimmed the top of my mind and picked off my wonderment at his telling me the story. Then I shook off the feeling and said, "That's understandable. If I ever *did* wonder about you and Mrs. Da Campo, well, it's something I won't do any more. And feel free to drop over any time you get the urge."

He looked thankful, as though I'd offered him the Northern Hemisphere, and stood up.

"Thanks a lot, John. I was hoping you'd understand."

We shook hands, I asked him if he wanted to call up the Missus and come over for dinner, but he said no thanks and we'd certainly get together again soon.

He left, and I wasn't surprised to see the cup of sugar sitting on an end table where he'd set it down.

Nice guy, I thought to myself.

Then I thought of that staring plant, which he hadn't explained at all, and some of the worry returned.

I shrugged it off. After three weeks I forgot it entirely. But Da Campo and I never got together as he'd suggested.

At least not at the Civic Center.

Da Campo kept going to the City on the 7:40 and coming back on the 5:35 every day. But somehow, we never sat together, and never spoke to one another. I made tentative gestures once or twice, but he indicated disinterest, so I stopped.

Ellie Da Campo would always be waiting at the station, parked a few cars down from Charlotte in her station wagon, and Clark Da Campo would pop into it and they'd be off before most of the rest of us were off the train.

I stopped wondering about the absence of light or life or smoke or anything else around the Da Campo household, figuring the guy knew what he was doing. I also took pains to caution Jamie to stay strictly off-limits, with or without baseball.

I also stopped wondering because I had enough headaches from the office to take full-time precedence on my brain-strain.

Then one morning, something changed my careful hands-off policies.

They had to change. My fingers were pushed into the pie forcibly.

I was worried sick over the Gillings business.

The Gillings Mills were trying to branch over into territory held by another of our Association's members, trying to buy timber land out from under the other. It looked like a drastic shake-up was in the near offing.

The whole miserable mess had been heaped on me, and I'd not only been losing my Saturdays—and a few Sundays to boot—but my hair was, so help me God, whitening, and the oculist said all the paperwork had played Hell with my eyes. I was sick to tears of the thing, but it was me all the way, and if I didn't play it right mergers might not merge, commitments might not be committed, and John Weiler might find himself on the outside.

Mornings on the train were a headache and a nightmare. Faces blurred into one runny grey smear, and the clickety-clack didn't carry me back. It made my head throb and my bones ache and it made me hate the universe. Not just the world—the *universe!* All of it.

I unzipped my briefcase and opened it on my lap. The balding $25,000-a-year man sharing the seat harrumphed once and gathered the folds of his Harris tweed about his paunch. He went back to the *Times* with a nasty side glance at me.

I mentally stuck my tongue out and bent to the paperwork.

I was halfway through an important field agent's report that might—just barely might—provide the loophole I was seeking to stop the gobbling by the Gillings Mills, and I walked out of the station with my briefcase under my arm, my nose in the report, with a sort of mechanical stride.

About halfway down the subway ramp I realized I didn't know where the bloody Hell I was. Hurrying men and women surrounded me, streaming like salmon heading to spawn. I was somewhere under Grand Central's teeming passageway labyrinth, heading for an exit that would bring me out into the street somewhere near my building.

But where the devil *was* this?

I'd never seen any of the signs on the tiled walls before. They were all in gibberish, but they seemed to be the usual type thing: women, big bold letters in some foreign language, packaged goods, bright colors.

I lost interest in them and tried to figure out where I was.

I'd gone up through the Station and then down again into the subway. Then there'd been a long period of walking while reading that damned report, and thinking my practiced feet knew where they were going.

It dawned on me that for the last few years I'd been

letting myself go where my feet led me each morning. Yeah, but my feet were following the subconscious orders of my head that said *follow the rest of the commuters*.

This morning I'd just followed the wrong batch.

A string of yellow lights spaced far apart in the ceiling, between the regular lights, indicated the way to a line of some sort. I followed the lights for a while until I looked down at my watch, for perhaps the hundredth time that morning, and realized it was past nine. I was late for the office.

Today of all days!

I started to get panicky and stopped a grey-suited man hurrying past with a sheaf of papers under his arm.

"Say, can you tell me where the exit onto 42nd and Lex—"

"Derlagos-km'ma-sne'ephor-july, esperind," he drawled out of the corner of his mouth and stalked past.

I was standing there stupidly till the next couple people cast dirty looks at me for being in the way.

Foreigner, I thought, and grabbed a girl who was walking with typical hurried secretarial steps. "Say, I'm trying to get out of here. Where's the 42nd and Lexington exit?"

She looked at me, amazedly, for a moment, shook my hand loose from her coat-sleeve, and pattered off, looking once over her shoulder. That look was a clear, "Are you nuts, Mac?"

I was getting really worried. I had no idea where the blazes I was, or where I was heading, or how to get out. I hadn't seen an exit in some time. And still the people continued to stream purposefully by me.

Subways had always scared me, but this was the capper.

Then I recognized the arrows on the wall. They were marked with the same kind of hyphenated, apostrophied anagrams on the billboards, but at least I got the message!

THIS WAY TO SOMEWHERE!

I followed the crowd.

By the time I got to the train, I was in the middle of a swarm of people, all madly pushing to get into the cars. "Hey, hold it! I don't want to—! Wait a minute!"

I was carried forward, pressed like a rose in a scrap-book, borne protesting through the doors of the car, and squashed up against the opposite door.

If you live in New York you will know this is not an impossibility. If you don't, take my word for it.

The doors slid shut with a pneumatic sigh and the train shot forward. Without a jar. That was when I began to sweat full-time.

I had wondered, sure, but in the middle of downtown Manhattan you just don't expect anything weird or out-of-place unless there's a press agent behind it. But this was no publicity stunt. Something was wrong. Way off-base wrong, and I was caught in the midst of it.

I wasn't scared, really, because I didn't know what there was to be afraid of, and there was too much familiarity about it all to hit me fully.

I had been in a million subway crushes just like this one. Had my glasses knocked off and trampled, had my suit wrinkled, had the shine taken off my shoes, too often to think there was anything untoward here.

But the signs had been in a foreign language. No one I'd been able to accost would talk to me in anything but gibberish, and most of them looked at me as though my skin was green. The train was definitely *not* an ordinary train. It had started without a jerking rasp. If you know New York subways, you know what I mean.

That was unusual. That was fantastic!

I bit my lower lip, elbowed my way into a relatively clear space in the car, and for the second time in my life dragged out my square-folded lapel hankie to mop my face.

Then I saw Da Campo.

He was sitting in one of the plush seats, reading a news-paper. The headline read:

SELFGEMMEN-BARNSNEBBLE   J'J'KEL-WOLO-BAGEDTAR!

I blinked. I blinked again. It was Da Campo all right, but that newspaper! What the Hell was it?

I made my way over to him, and tapped him on the shoulder, "Say, Da Campo, how the deuce do I—"

"Good Tilburr all mighty!" he squawked, his eyes bug-ging, the newspaper falling to the floor. "How the—dwid olu—did you follow—Weiler!" He went off in a burst of that strange gibberish, gasped, and finally got out, "What are you doing here, for God's sake, man?"

"Look, Da Campo, I got lost in the subway. Took a wrong turn or something. All I want is out of here. Where's this train's next stop?"

"Drexwill, you damned fool!"

"Is that anywhere near Westchester?"

"It's so far away your best telescopes don't even know it exists!" He was getting red in the face.

"What?"

"The planet Drexwill, you idiot! What the Hell are you doing here?"

I felt suddenly choked, hemmed in, like a fist was tightening around the outside of my head, squeezing it.

"Look, Da Campo, this isn't funny. I've got an appointment this morning, and the office is waiting for me to——"

"Understand this, Weiler!" he snapped, pointing a finger that seemed to fill the universe for me. "You'll never make that appointment!"

"But why? I can get off at the next sta——"

"You'll never make another appointment back there." His eyes flicked back toward the rear of the car and I found my own drawn in that direction. The fear was crawling around in me like a live thing.

He seemed to be grinding inside. His face was screwed up in an expression of distaste, disbelief and pity. "Why? Why? Why didn't you leave well enough alone? Why couldn't you believe what I told you and not follow me?" His hands made futile gestures, and I saw the people near us suddenly come alive with the same expressions as our conversation reached them.

I was into something horrible, and I didn't know precisely what!

"Auditor! Auditor! Is there an Auditor in the car?" yelled Da Campo, twisting around in his seat.

"Da Campo, what are you doing? Help me, get me off this train, I don't know where I'm going, and I have to be at the office!" I was getting hysterical, and Da Campo kept looking from me to the back of the car, screaming for an Auditor, whatever that was.

"I can't help you, Weiler, I'm just like you. I'm just another commuter like you, only I go a little further to work every day."

The whole thing started to come to me then, and the idea, the very concept, dried my throat out, made my brain ache.

"Auditor! Auditor!" Da Campo kept yelling.

A man across the aisle leaned over and said something in that hyphenated gibberish, and Da Campo's lips became a thin line. He looked as though he wanted to slap his forehead in frustration.

"There isn't one on the train. This is the early morning local." He made fists, rubbed the thumbs over the tightened fingers.

A sign began flashing on and off, on and off, in yellow letters, over the door of the car, and everyone lowered his newspaper with a bored and resigned expression.

The sign blinked HUL-HUBBER on and off.

"Translation," said Da Campo briefly, and then the car turned inside out.

Everything went black and formless and limp in the car and for a split split-second my intestines were sloshing around in the crown of my hat and my shoe soles were stuck to my upper lip. Then the lights came back on, everyone lifted his paper, the sign went dead, and I felt as though I wanted to vomit.

"Good Lord above, what was *that?*" I gasped, holding onto the back of Da Campo's seat.

"Translation," he said simply, and went back to his paper.

I suddenly became furious. Here I was lost in a subway, going—if I was to believe what I had been told—somewhere called Drexwill. I was late for the office, and this thing had overtones that were only now beginning to shade in with any sort of logic. A mad sort of logic, but logic nonetheless.

And the only person I knew here was reading his newspaper as though my presence was a commonplace thing.

"Da Campo!" I screamed, knocking the weird newspaper out of his hands. Heads turned in annoyance. "Do something! Get me off this goddamed thing!"

I grabbed his coat lapel, but he slapped my hand away.

"Look, Weiler, you got yourself into this, you'll just have to wait till we hit the Depot and we can fish out an Auditor to help you.

"I'm just a lousy businessman; I can't handle anything

as snarled as this. This is government business, and it's your headache, not mine. I have to be at work . . ."

I wasn't listening. It all shaded in properly. I saw the picture. I didn't know where I was going, or what it was like there, but I knew why Da Campo was on this train, and what he'd been doing in my town.

I wanted to cry out because it was so simple.

I wanted to cry because it was so simply terrifying.

The train slowed, braked, and came to a hissing halt, without lurching. The doors opened and the many commuterly-dressed people who had been crowded into the car began to stream out. The entire trip couldn't have taken more than twenty minutes.

Then I thought of that "translation" and I wasn't so sure of my time estimate.

"Come on," said Da Campo, "I'll get you to an Auditor." He glanced down at his wrist, frowning at the dial of a weirdly-numeraled watch. He whistled through his teeth for a moment, as the crowd pushed out. Then he shoved me after them resignedly. "Let's hurry," he said, "I haven't much time."

He herded me before him, and told me to wait a moment while he took care of something. He stepped to the end of a line of men and women about to enter a small booth, one of about twenty such booths. A dilating opening in the booth admitted one person at a time.

In a few moments the line had diminished, as men went in one side wearing suits like my own grey flannel, and emerged from the other clad in odd, short jackets and skin-tight pants. The women came out in the equivalent, only tailored for the female form. They didn't look bad at all.

Da Campo went in and quickly came out. He stepped to my side, dressed like the others, and began pushing me again.

"Had to change for work," he commented shortly. "Come on."

I followed him, confused. My stomach was getting more and more uneasy. I had a feeling that the twinge I'd occasionally felt in my stomach was going to develop into an ulcer.

We stepped onto an escalator-like stairway that carried

us up through a series of floors where I saw more people —dressed like Da Campo—scurrying back and forth. "Who are they?" I asked.

Da Campo looked at me with pity and annoyance and said, "Commuters."

"Earth is a suburb, isn't it?" I asked.

He nodded, not looking at me.

I knew what it was all about, then. A fool would be the only one unable to see the picture after all the pieces had been laid out so clearly. It was really quite simple:

Earth was being infiltrated. But there wasn't any sinister invasion or displacement afoot. That was ridiculous. The only reason these aliens were on Earth was to live.

When I thought the word "alien" I looked at Da Campo. He appeared to be the same as anyone of Earth. These "aliens" were obviously exactly like us, physically. Physically.

Why were the aliens on Earth to live? Again, simple.

Why does a man who works in New York City go out to Westchester after 5:00 every day? Answer: the city is too crowded. He goes to the suburbs to live quietly.

"Is—uh—Drexwill crowded, Da Campo? I mean, are there a lot of people here?"

He nodded again and muttered something about serious over-population and why didn't the stupid Faenalists use their heads and bring things under control and wasn't that what he was paying his Allotments for.

The escalator was coming to another floor, and Da Campo made movements toward the exit side. He stepped off, and I followed. He gave me a quick glance to make sure I was following, and strode briskly away.

All around us people were coming and going with quiet purpose.

"Da Campo—" I began, trying to get his attention. His nonchalance and attitude of trying to brush me off were beginning to terrify me more than all the really strange things going on around me.

"Stop calling me that, you fool! My name is Helgorth Labbula, and if you refer to me again with that idiotic name I'll leave you here and let you fend for yourself. I'm only taking my time to get you to an Auditor because they might construe it as my fault that you wandered into the Suburb Depot." He glared at me, and I bit my lip.

We kept walking and I wondered what an Auditor was, and where we were going to find one.

I found out quickly enough. Da Cam—er, Helgorth Labbula spotted a tall, hard-looking man in a deep blue version of the universal short jacket and tight pants, and hailed him.

The Auditor walked over and Da Campo talked to him in soft tones for a moment. I watched as the man's eyes got wider and wider, as Da Campo's talk progressed.

"Hey!" I yelled. They both looked up, annoyed.

"I hate to say anything," I said, "but if I'm right, you're talking about me, and I don't like this cold-shoulder routine, not one little bit." I was sick of all this rigamarole, and me stuck somewhere a million miles or more away from my office, and everyone acting as though I'd done it on purpose and I was a nuisance.

"Now talk in English so I can understand, will you?"

The Auditor turned cool grey eyes on me. Stiffly, as though he were unaccustomed to speaking the language, he said, "You have stumbled into something by chance, and though it is not your fault, dispensation must be arranged. Will you please come with me."

He stated it, didn't ask it, and I had no choice.

We took a few steps, and the Auditor turned to stare back at Da Campo who was watching us balefully. "You, too," the man in the blue tunic said.

"But I have to be at—"

"You will be needed for a statement. I'm sorry, but it's official."

"What am I paying my Allotments for, if you Auditors can't handle a little thing like this?" He was getting angry, but the Auditor shrugged his shoulders, and Da Campo trudged along behind us.

We came up off one of the escalators, into the light of triple suns. Three of them. Burning all at once. Triple shadows. That was when I realized how far away, more than a mere million miles, and how strange, and how lost I was.

"How—how far from Earth are we?" I asked.

The Auditor answered absently, "About 60,000 light-years."

I gawked, stopped dead in my tracks. "But you toss

it off so lightly, as though it were around the block! And
you don't live that differently from us! I don't understand!"

"Understand? What's to understand?" snapped Da
Campo with annoyance. "It was a fluke that discovered
Translation, and allowed us to live off Drexwill. But it
didn't change our culture much. Why *shouldn't* we take
it for granted? We've lived with it all our lives, and
there's nothing odd or marvelous about it."

"In fact," he added, glaring at the Auditor, "it's a
blasted bother sometimes!"

His tossing it off in that manner only made it worse for
me.

I thought of the distance between me and my office,
realizing I hadn't the faintest idea how far away it was,
but knowing it was further than anything I could ever
imagine. I tried putting it into mundane terms by re-
membering that the nearest star to Earth was only four
light-years away and then trying something like:

*If all the chewing-gum wrappers in the world were
laid end to end, they'd stretch from Earth to—*

But it only made things worse.

I was lost.

"I want to go home," I said, and realized I sounded
like a little boy. But I couldn't help it.

The Auditor and Da Campo turned to look at me at
the same time. I wished I had been unable to read what
was in their eyes.

But I could. I wished I hadn't been able to, really.

They hurried me down a street, if street it was, and I
supposed that was what it was, and into a bubble-like car
with a blue insignia, that sat by the curb. It ran on a
monorail, and in a few seconds we had left the Depot
behind.

We sped through the city, and oddly, I didn't marvel
at the fantastic architecture and evidences of great
science, though there were enough of both. From the
screaming ships that split the morning sky to the cone-
within-helix buildings rising on all sides.

I didn't look, because it was so restful for the first
time in my life not to have to worry about offices, and
commuting, and bills, and Charlotte's ashtray fetish, or
any of the other goddam bothers I had been heir to since

I was able to go out and earn a living. No treadmill. No responsibility.

It was good to lie back in the padded seat and just close my eyes. Even though I knew I was in deep trouble.

We drove for a while, and then something occurred to me.

"Why don't we just translate where we're going?"

The Auditor was looking out the window abstractedly, but he said, "Too short a jump. It only works in light-year minimums."

"Oh," I said, and sank back again.

It was all so logical.

Something else popped into my mind. The sheet of liabilities under my desk blotter.

"Uh—Da Campo," I began, and shrank back at the scathing look he turned on me.

"The name is Helgorth Labbula, I told you!"

The Auditor smiled out the window.

"Want to tell me a few things?" I asked, timidly.

Da Campo sighed once, deeply, "Go ahead. You can't be any more trouble to me than you have already. I'm twenty kil-boros late already."

"What was that in your garden?"

"A plant, what do you think?"

"But—"

He seemed about to explode with irritation. "Look, Weiler, you grow those runty little chrysanthemums and roses, don't you? Well, why shouldn't I be entitled to grow a native plant in my garden? Just because I'm living out there in the sticks doesn't mean I have to act and live like a barbarian."

The Auditor looked over, "Yes, but you were warned several times about growing native plants in Suburb Territory when you signed the real estate release, weren't you, Helgorth?"

Da Campo turned red.

"Well, that's—what I mean is—a man has to have *some*—" He stuttered into silence and looked at me with wrath.

"How come we never saw any smoke from your house?"

"We don't use imbecilic fuels like coal or gas or oil."

I didn't understand, but he cleared it up with the answer to my next question. I said, "Why don't you ever go out, or show lights at night, and why do you pull those drapes?"

"Because the inside of our house isn't like yours. We have a Drexwillian bungalow in there. A bit cramped for space we are," he said, casting a nasty look at the Auditor, "but with regulations what they are, we can't expect much better. We have our own independent heating system, food supply, lighting system and everything else. We pull the drapes so you won't see when we turn on all the units at once. We have to inconvenience ourselves, I'll tell you.

"But at least it's better than living in this madhouse," he finished, waving a hand at the bustling city.

"I rather like it," I said.

The Auditor glanced over at me again, and for the second time I read his eyes. The message hadn't changed. I was still in trouble.

"We're almost there," he said.

The car slowed and came to an easy stop before a huge white building, and we got out.

Da Campo held back and spoke to the Auditor again in tones that indicated he wanted to leave.

"It will only take a short time. We need your statement," the Auditor told him, motioning him out of the car.

We walked up the wide, resilient steps.

After a wearying progression through the stages of red tape, statements, personnel, and official procedure which reminded me strongly of Earth, we came to an office that seemed to be the end of the road.

Da Campo was uneasy and kept damning me with his eyes when he wasn't looking at his watch.

We were ushered in, and the Auditor saluted the pale-faced man behind the desk. "The Head Auditor," said the blue-uniformed man, and left us. I noticed that the official had grey eyes, like Da Campo and the Auditor. Was that a dominant on Drexwill?

"Sit down, won't you?" he said, amiably enough.

Da Campo blurted, "I really must be going. I'm quite late for my work and if you don't mind I'd like to—"

"*Sit*, Helgorth, I have something to say to you, too."

I was grateful they were speaking English.

The Head Auditor crossed long arms and glared at Da Campo across the desk.

"You know you're partially to fault here."

Da Campo was indignant. "Why—why—what do you mean? I gave him a perfectly logical story, but he had to go and stumble into the Suburb Depot. That wasn't my—"

"Quiet! We leave you commuters pretty much alone. It's your lives and we try not to meddle. But there are certain regulations we have to keep enforced or the entire system will break down.

"You knew you weren't to grow any native plants out there. We warned you enough times so that it should have made an impression. Then to boot, you became a recluse out there. We ask you to make certain advances to your neighbors, strictly for purposes of keeping things on a level. But you wouldn't even go shopping!"

Da Campo started to protest, but the Head Auditor snapped his fingers sharply, causing the man to fall silent. "We checked your supply requisitions through Food Central, and we were going to drop you a memo on it, but we didn't get to it in time."

The pale-faced man tapped his fingers on the desk, "Now if we have any more trouble out of you, Helgorth, we're going to yank your Suburb Ticket and get you and your wife back into one of the Community Towers. Is that clear?"

Da Campo, suitably cowed, merely nodded.

I thought of the fantastic system they had devised. All Earth turned into a suburban development. Lord! It was fantastic, yet so simple and so obvious when I thought about it, my opinion of these people went up more and more. This explained all sorts of things I'd wondered about: hermits, bus lines that went nowhere, people disappearing.

"All right, you can go," I heard the Head Auditor say.

Da Campo got up to leave, and I turned to watch him. "So long, Da Campo, see you at home tonight," I said.

He looked at me strangely. The message hadn't altered. "So long, Weiler. I hope so," he said, and was gone.

I half-knew what he meant.

They weren't going to let me go back. That would be foolish. I knew too much. Strangely, I felt no fear.

"You see our predicament, don't you?" asked the Head Auditor, and I swung back to look at him. I must have looked at him in amazement, because he added, "I couldn't help knowing what you were thinking."

I nodded, reaching for a way to say what I wanted to say.

"We can't let you go back."

"Fine," I smiled a bit too eagerly. "Let me stay. I'd like to stay here. You can't imagine how fascinated I am by your planet."

And it was then, right in that instant, that I recognized the truth in what I'd said.

I hated Earth.

I hated the nine-to-five drudgery of the closed office and the boring men and women with whom I did business.

I despised my wife, who wanted More. And Better. And More Expensive. I realized how I'd been fooled by her flippant and sometimes affectionate attitude. I was a faceless thing to her. A goddam man in a grey flannel suit.

I despised the trains and the vacuum cleaners and the routine. I despised the lousy treadmill!

I loathed, detested, despised, abhorred, abominated and in all *hated* the miserable system. I didn't *want* to go back.

"I don't *want* to go back! I want to stay. Let me stay here!"

The Head Auditor was shaking his auditing head.

"Why not?" I asked, confused.

"Look, we're overpopulated now! Why do you think we use the Suburbs out there? There isn't room here for anyone like you. We have enough non-working bums on our hands without you. Just because you stumbled into one of our Depots, don't assume we owe you anything. Because we don't.

"No, I'm afraid we'll have to—er—dispense with you, Mr. Weiler. We're not unpleasant people, but there is a point where we must stand and say, 'No more!' I'm sorry." He started to push a button.

I went white. I could feel myself going white. *Oh no,* I thought! I've got to talk!

So I talked. I talked him away from that button, because I suppose he had a wife and children and didn't really like killing people. And I talked him away from the killing angle entirely. And I talked and talked and talked till my throat was dry and he threw up his hand and said . . .

"All right, all right, *stop!* A trial, then. If you can find work here, if you can fit in, if you can match up, there's no reason why you shouldn't stay. But don't ever expect to go back!"

Expect to go back? Not on your life!

Then he shooed me out of the office, and I set about making a place for myself in this world I'd never made.

Well, I've done pretty decently. I'm happy, I have my own apartment, and I have a good job. They've said I can stay.

I didn't realize it, all those years, how much I hated the rush, rush, rush, the getting to the office and poring over those lousy briefs, the quiet nagging of Charlotte about things like the ashtrays, the constant bill collectors, the keeping up with the Joneses.

I didn't realize how badly I wanted out.

Well, now I'm out, and I'm happy. No more of that stuff for me.

Thanks for listening. Thought I'd get it straight, as long as you needed the story to open my charge account. I'm here and I like it, and I'm out of the suburbanite climbing-executive rush-rush class. At last I'm off that infernal treadmill.

Thanks again for listening. Well, I've got to go.

Got to get to work, you know.

Current crazes fascinate me. Though I couldn't operate one to save my life, the hula hoop was an entrancing little path to dislocation of the spine and ultimate madness, and I watched with not too much lasciviousness as the pre-adult vixens of my acquaintance shimmied and swirled in the use of same. The telephone-booth-stuffing trend seemed to me abortive, and I was not at all surprised when it faded in lieu of the "limbo" acrobatics at voodoo calypso parties. Mah-jongg, Scrabble, ouija boards, Lotto, TV quiz shows, pennies in kids' loafers, bongo boards, snake dances, panty raids, rumble seats, trampoline classes, croquet, Empire-line dresses, day-glo shirts, stuffed tigers in car back windows, Billy Graham and Fabian (no relation)—all of them awed and bemused me, as I watched the world swallow them whole, digest them and infuse them into the daily scene. Trends knock me out, frankly: Whether it be painting by the numbers or making your own full-scale skeleton of a tyrannosaurus, I think the most imaginative, and auctorially-useful fad of recent years has been the one aptly called

do-it-yourself

Madge retina-printed her identity on the receipt, fished in her apron for a coin, and came up with a thirty-center. It was a bit too much to give the boy, but she already had it in her hand, and there *were* appearances to keep up, in spite of everything. She handed it across, and took the carton.

A migrant tremor of pleasure swept her as she was closing the door; the messenger boy was assaying her figure. It had been years, oh longer than that, since a young man had done that. Perhaps it was the new wash; she closed the door firmly and blanked it, patting her hair. Yes, it was the blonde rinse, that was it.

Abruptly, she realized she had been standing there, staring at the box in her hands, for some time. With mild terror.

Madge Rubichek, she chided herself, *you contracted for this, and now it's here, and it's paid for, so what are you making faces like that for? Go in and sit down and open it, you silly goose!*

She followed her silent instructions. In the kitchen, with the late afternoon operock program from Philly weirdly jangling the background—they were doing the new two-beat *La Forza del Destino* with alto sax accompaniment—she took a paring knife—my, how infectious that sort of teen-ager's music was!—to the thick, white scotchseal of the carton.

The box was secured around the edges, and she inserted the paring knife as she would have with a carton of soda crackers. She slit it open down one side, up the next.

Except this was not a carton of soda crackers.

This was—oh, how odd—a do-it-yourself kit. A modern marvel like all the new do-it-yourself marvels. Do-it-yourself house painting setups, and do-it-yourself baked Alaska mix, and do-it-yourself this and that and the other thing. There were even advertisements for do-it-yourself brain surgery kits and swamp digging kits, for chassis aligning kits and pruning kits. But this was no longer something offered in an advertisement; once it had been, but now it was a reality, and she held it in her hands. As much of that advertised breed as any do-it-yourself bookcase-construction kit, outfitted to the last set screw.

This was a particular *kind* of kit Madge had purchased:

To be precise, a do-it-yourself murder kit.

Idly, as though without conscious direction, her eyes strayed to the magazine spindle where DO-IT-YOUR-SELF MONTHLY was canned up against Carl's FLIK-PIX and her own mundane BEST HOUSEKEEPING. Her eyes lingered for an instant, drank in through the impeding plastic of the container and the other spools the classified advertisement near the end of the mag-reel . . . and passed on around the room.

It was a nice room. A solid room, furnished in tasteful period furniture without too many curlicues and just enough modern angles. But it was mediocrity, and what else was there to say of it but that it typified her life with Carl. Mediocrity disturbed Madge Rubichek, as did the slovenly day-to-day existence of her husband.

For Madge Rubichek was a methodical woman.

She sighed resignedly, and busied herself lifting the top from the carton. It was a long, moderately-thin package, of typical brown box-plastboard. Her name had been neatly *stat*ed on the address label, and there was no return address.

"Well, impractical, but necessary," she mused, aloud, "but what a lot of merchandise they must lose," she added. Then it dawned on her that she had signed a return receipt, and that meant the boy who had come to the door must have gotten the carton from a central delivery robotic mailer, or else . . .

Oh, it was too deep for her to worry about. They must have *some* way of insuring delivery. She set the box top beside her chair, and pulled away the tissue paper double-folded over the carton's contents.

What odd-looking mechanisms. Even for 1977, which Madge had always called—in the sanctum of her mind, where profanity was permitted—"too damned machiney for its own good!" these were strange.

There was a long, thin, coiled sticky-looking tube of grey something-or-other with a valve at one end, and a blow-nozzle attached. Was it one of those dragon balloons that you blew up so big? But what did that have to do with—

She would not think of what this kit had been invented to do. She would look at it as though it were some labor-saving household appliance, like her Dinner Dialer (that did not dial at all, but was punched, instead) or her Dustomat. Well, and she giggled, *wasn't* it?

Do-it-by-golly-yourself!

Beside the coil of grey tubing, hooked to it by soft wire and wrapped in tissue paper like a Christmas necklace, was another small parcel. She lifted it out, surprised at its heaviness, and stripped away the tissue.

It was a small glass square, obviously a bottle of some sort, filled with a murky, mercurial-seeming liquid that moved rapidly as she turned the container, sending up no air bubbles as it roiled in the bottle. It had a tiny, pin-like protuberance at one corner, with a boot fastened down on it, easily snapped off to open the vial. Quicksilver? She found this item as mystifying as the preceding one. She stared at it a moment longer, with no apparent function coming to mind, and then she laid it aside.

It slipped down behind the chair's pillow, and she retrieved it at once, without examining the carton further.

Madge Rubichek was a methodical woman.

The next was a layer in itself; rather thick and quite black, it was almost of the consistency of an old beach ball, or a fish skin without scales, or—

What?

Rotten flesh . . . perhaps. Though she had no conception of what rotten flesh felt like. Or something.

She pulled it free, and almost immediately let it drop into the leaning carton top beside her chair. She just didn't want to *touch* it. Mental images of dead babies and salamanders and polyethylene bags filled with vomit came to mind when her fingers touched that night-black stuff.

She dropped it free, and found beneath it a pamphlet without a title, and a small glass globe with all the attributes of a snowstorm paperweight, the kind her Grandfather had had on his desk in the old law offices in Prestonsburg. It was on an onyx stand of some cheap material, and the globe itself swirled and frothed with the artificial whateveritwas inside. But there was no little town once the snow settled, and no large-thoraxed snowman with anthracite eyes, and no church. There was nothing in there but the lacy swirlingness. The snow just continued to whirl about, no matter how long it lay in one position. It would not settle.

She put it beside her on the chair, and nudged the carton, now empty, off her lap. She took the pamphlet in her hands, and opened it to the first page.

"Hello," it said.

It did not *read* hello, it *said* hello. In a rich baritone, vaguely reminiscent of old-fashioned styrene records she had heard of pressings taken off even older platters made by Peter Ustinov, a mimic comedian of the Fifties. It was in many ways a comforting voice, and one that was subtly reassuring, as well as inviting attention and forthrightness of manner, clarity of thinking, boldness of approach.

It was a mellow and warm voice.

It was, apparently, the voice of murder.

"Hello," it said again, and this time there was a tinge of apprehension in its voice, as though it was not certain there was anyone on the holding end of the pamphlet.

"Uh, hello," she replied, not at all certain it was good taste to be conversing with a pamphlet. There was, in fact, a sense of Carrollian madness about it. Had a Dormouse erupted from the delicate Chinese teapot on the coffee table before the sofa, clearly enunciating *Twinkle, twinkle, little bat* . . . she would not have been overly surprised; it would have fitted in nicely.

"This is your own Do-It-Yourself Murder Kit," the pamphlet broke her literary reverie with harsh reality. "The *new* guaranteed Murder Kit, with the double-your-money-back warranty, for your protection."

Well, she thought, frugally, *that's nice, anyway. That double-your-money-back thing.* She shivered a little with suppressed anticipation. There was going to be profit . . . one way . . . or the other.

"Uh, where are you?" Madge asked nervously.

"Where am I *where?*" the pamphlet responded in confusion.

"Yes, precisely," she concurred.

"Dear Purchaser, you are perplexing me," cried the pamphlet. "If you wish to carry forward smartly to the objective for which this Kit was designed, please do not strain my conversational and analytical faculties."

"But I only—"

"Madam, if you desire success, you must put yourself wholly in my—er—hands. Do I make myself clear?"

Madge drew herself up, and an expression of haughty resignation suffused her face. "I understand quite well, thank you." After all, Grandfather Tabakow on her mother's side had been Southern aristocracy, well *hadn't* he? She felt imposed upon, this mere booklet talking to her that way.

And a booklet without even the common self-respect of having a title. After all, a *title*-less pamphlet.

And wasn't the customer always supposed to be right? It didn't seem so with this Kit.

The phrase *nouveau-riche* flitted across Madge's mind, with ill-concealed contempt.

"This guaranteed Murder Kit," the voice continued, "was shipped to you by our robotic mailer. There is no record of its sale in our hands. So in case you wish to exercise the warranty you must return the numbered warranty sheet on the last page of this pamphlet. To return the numbered warranty sheet to our files, merely burn same in a non-chemical fire; this will automatically cancel the sympathetic-sheet in our files, and your money will be doubly, cheerfully refunded.

"This Kit contains three sure, clean and undetectable, I repeat, *undetectable,* ways to commit murder. No two kits are the same, though repetition occasionally occurs where the subjects to be murdered have common character traits. Again, though, no two kits are the same. Each of the three *modus operandi* is designed for you according to the application blank you sent us when you contracted for this Kit. Now. To prepare yourself for your murder—"

She snapped the pamphlet shut with quick, suddenly-sweating hands.

Do I hate him that much?

Where had their marriage gone wrong . . . somewhere in the eleven years? Where? An infinite sadness stole over her as she remembered Carl the way he had been when they first met. She remembered his ways, that had seemed rough and yet gentle, masculine yet graceful. And she recalled her own aristocratic nature, the fine background, and the womanly ways. But how had it changed? How was it now?

She conjured up visions of it now. The ashes on the carpets and the smell of musty cigar smoke that stayed in the curtains and chair coverings no matter how much she aired and cleaned. She remembered the fat, nasty belly of the man while he sat pouring bock down his dribble-chinned throat, the clothes rank with sweat strewn across her immaculate bedroom, the rings in the bathtub, his rotten teeth and the odor when he kissed her . . .

And of course the quick animal urges all panting and grunting that were as nothing to her. Nothing but revulsion.

She answered her question firmly: *Yes, yes, I hate him that much. And more!*

She opened the pamphlet again. Her hands had become dry and almost cool again.

"The first method of murder we have prepared for you," the pamphlet's voice continued, undaunted, "is the rabid dog method. You will notice a coil of grey substance. This is your Animaux Tube. Warning is issued at this point that instructions throughout the use of this Kit must be *specifically* followed, or failure will result. There is no mechanical failure possible with this Kit, only *human* failure through inefficiency and disregard of stated operating procedures. Is this understood?"

"Yes, I suppose so," Madge answered, surlily.

"With your Animaux Tube, attached by wire, is a vial of Essence, a specially-produced, copyrighted substance to be used *only* with the Animaux Tube. Again warning is issued to preclude any ill-use of materials included in your Kit. Unspecified use of the Essence included in your Kit will prove most unpleasant. In the human digestive tract it reacts violently, causing almost immediate convulsions and death. Care should be exercised to keep the vial away from children and pets."

She lifted the coil of stuff and it *was* sticky. After spreading a sheet of newsfax on the rug, she allowed the grey tubing to unroll itself out onto the fax sheet. There was no sense ruining a good rug with any odd chemicals from this Kit. She had always been a methodically neat woman, and just because she was doing what she was doing, was no reason to become a crude slob—like Carl.

The coil unrolled and it had queer blotches on it, almost like military camouflage canvas. What it was, she still could not ascertain.

"Take some article of clothing belonging to the intended victim," the pamphlet voice continued, startling her, "and place a small piece of it firmly against the Animaux Tube, on the orange blotch near its front. Press it, and it will adhere. Then inflate the Tube by blowing gently and evenly into the nozzle. Only after the Animaux Tube has been inflated should the Essence then be added. Screw the vial of Essence onto the air valve and allow it to drain completely into the Animaux Tube. Make certain that every drop enters. You will then have your Animaux rabid dog. Set the dog loose when the intended victim is near and it will inflict a bite wound that cannot be cured by regular methods; a bite wound that will cause violent death within a matter of minutes."

She used one of his socks, holding it as far away from her as possible. It was hideously pungent and ripe after only one wearing. The dog itself took shape quickly. The

Tube seemed to retain the air blown into it; there was no blowback.

The surge of anticipation turned her hands clumsy when she hooked the Essence to the blown-up Tube and a few drops spilled onto the newsfax underneath it.

The thing moved softly. It looked for all the world like a medium-sized mongrel dog of no apparent lineage.

It limped toward the door and stood there whining, its jaws slavering hideously.

"Not for a few more minutes," she told it soothingly, afraid of it herself, yet exhilarated by what she was doing, what was to be done soon enough. "He won't be getting off the slipway for a few minutes." She spent the time neatly hiding the rest of the Kit and the now-silent pamphlet in her clothes closet, at the bottom of a moth-proof garment safette. Then, when it was time, she let the dog out.

Carl came gruffily into the house, cursing foully, and her heart sank.

The hairy arms surrounded her like a scratching womb, and she stood passively hoping for a blast of lightning that would char him on the spot, and *damn* the rug damage! She could smell his teeth rotting in his head.

"Damn dog tried t'bite me when I got offa the express-walk. Thing musta been sick." He nodded proudly, "Kicked it an' the sonofabitch died right there. Real soggy mess," and he laughed imbecilically. "Never even touched me."

The next morning, as soon as he had slipped to work, as soon as she had watched the slipway carry him out of sight over the horizon to the Bactericidal Dome, she went to get the Do-It-Yourself Murder Kit. She took the Kit from its hiding place at the bottom of the moth-proof garment safette, and carried it into the dining nook. She was really annoyed; this Kit had not cost a pittance, and she wanted value for her money.

She punched herself a second cup of coffee—black with Saccha—and opened the pamphlet again.

"If you failed," the booklet began, as though anticipating her anger, "it was, as I warned you, through human error, and not on the part of this Kit. Was your murder a success?"

"No!" she answered, in a consummate pique.

The pamphlet was silent for an instant, as though refraining from taking offense. Then it began: "If you have not succeeded, attribute your failure to one of the following:

"One. You snagged your Animaux Tube and it was not fully inflated, or later lost air.

"Two. You did not allow the Essence to fill the Tube completely. Perhaps you spilled a portion.

"Three. You prepared your rabid dog for the scent improperly.

"Four. You did not attach your Essence vial properly, causing irreparable damage from leakage.

"Well, does one of these fit your case?"

The pamphlet waited, and she remembered the few drops of substance that had trickled free in her eagerness to set the dog loose on Carl. She mumbled something.

"What?" asked the pamphlet.

"I said: I spilled some!" she confessed loudly, shamefacedly, toying with the sip-tip of her coffee bulb.

"Ah so," the pamphlet agreed. "Undoubtedly, certain vital organs were not properly formed and stabilized, thus causing a malfunction of the pseudo-beast."

Recollections formed of the evening before, and she saw the rabid animal again, froth dripping from its viciously-spiked jaws . . . limping and whining. So *that* was it. Well, it wouldn't happen again. She would follow the instructions more carefully in the future.

Madge Rubichek was a methodical woman.

"What do I do now?" she asked.

The pamphlet seemed to make a snickering sound, as if it were acknowledging her loss of annoyance at it, and her own recognized sense of failure, her inferiority. It might be said the pamphlet was its own brand of snob.

Then its snideness disappeared, and the booklet advised, "Remove the Deadly Nightshade from your Kit. Be careful *not* to spread it out. Repeat, do *not* unfold it!"

She knew at once what was meant. The black sheet with the horrible feeling of dead flesh.

She hesitated to touch it, so repulsive was the tactile impression it offered; nonetheless, she reached into the

Kit and brought out the layer of softly-folded, unbelievably black, ghastly-feeling material. She dropped it at her feet.

"Are you ready?" asked the pamphlet.

She started violently. It was uncanny the way that thing knew what and when and how and oh well . . . it was *supposed* to, wasn't it? But so *creepy!*

"Yes, thank you."

"Excellent. Now this second method allows less room for human error. However, it is more dangerous, and more complex. Your three methods of murder are offered in order of increasing effort and danger. Sequentially, they are held so the simplest can be allowed to work first, thus denying the element of failure and discovery as much as possible.

"Your Deadly Nightshade is nearly flawless. If you follow my instructions to the exact letter *precisely*—and I cannot stress this enough—you will have accomplished your desire by morning.

"Your Deadly Nightshade is a copyrighted, patented—" and it reeled off, in a bored voice, a string of Guatemalan Patent Authority designates, "—exclusive with the Do-It-Yourself Murder Kit." She realized at once that the voice was huckstering out of necessity, that it found such commercialism odious, vulgar and tedious.

"It will provide night," the pamphlet said. "Night for the purpose you seek. Here is how it is used:

"Place it in the bedroom of the one you wish to eliminate. It is very important that this be done precisely as directed. On no account should you, after placing the Deadly Nightshade in the bedroom, re-enter it before the intended victim. The Deadly Nightshade acts as a controlled form of narcolepsy, by the release of hypnotically-keyed visual and mental depressents. The intended victim is cast into a hypnotic spell of long night. In three days he or she will *sleep* all life away. The room will be a place of perpetual darkness to him or her and slowly the vital bodily functions will fail and cease, beginning with the flow of blood to the brain.

"However, it is very important that you place the Nightshade in the intended's room evenly and without wrinkles, stretching it out under the bed or somewhere else where it will escape observation. And . . . you must *not* re-enter the room once you have placed the Deadly Nightshade. Exposure begins once the sheet is spread."

She shook it out like a chenille bedspread and laid it out neatly, placing it very carefully under the bed, once again precautionarily laying out newsfax to avoid any later unpleasantness to the floor. She tidied the bed, tucking nicely, the blankets as tight as those on the bunk of an army King/Sgt. She spread the Deadly Nightshade in a tight, wrinkle-free sheet.

She missed seeing the socks, somehow.

They were on the floor, just peeping out from under the bed, half-under the Deadly Nightshade.

She caught them out of the corner of her eye, just as she pulled the door to behind herself.

Carl's filthy, filthy socks. A pang of hysteria went through her. He always left them where they fell. She could not understand how she had failed to see them when she had tidied that morning, nor more important, when she had stretched out the Deadly Nightshade. Perhaps the excitement of the night before, and the fervor of now.

She remembered the instructions clearly.

"*. . . you must not re-enter the room once you have placed the Deadly Nightshade. Exposure begins once the sheet is spread . . .*"

Well! She certainly wasn't going to chance *that*.

As it was, she would have to invent a reason for coming to bed after he had retired. Perhaps the Midnight Movie on tri-V.

Nor was she going to foul it up as she had with the Animaux Tube. But just the same . . . those stinking socks.

On a level far deeper than any conscious urge to murder Carl, the training of a lifetime, the murmured words of her Mother, and the huge distaste of her Father for litter, sent her to the broom closet.

She re-opened the door, and yes . . . just by holding the broom tightly at the sucker-straws, by keeping her wrist flexed and tight to maintain rigid balanced control, she was able to snag the socks, one by one.

—and withdraw them.

—without entering the room.

—and close the door again.

Madge congratulated herself, once she had slung the

stench-filled socks into the dispop. She busied herself in the kitchen, punching out a scrumptious frappé dessert for Carl's dinner. His last dinner on this Earth. Or anywhere.

Not that he'd notice, the big boob, not that he'd notice.

Nor did *she* notice the great wrinkle in one end of the Deadly Nightshade. Caused by the prodding of the broom handle.

He was yawning, and it looked like the eroded south forty getting friendly.

"Jeezus, Madge honey, I nearly overslept. Whyn'tcha wake me? I'll be late for my shift."

She gawked, stricken. Twice!

"I ain't never seen nothin' like it, honey. I was enjoyin' the best sleep of my life, but this here bright, real bright streak of light was in my dreams, y'know? An' I couldn't rest easy, y'know. I kept squintin' and tossin' and finally hadda get up, cause I mean, Jeezus, it was painful. Piercin', y'know? So I got up, an' a lucky thing, too, or I'd'a missed my shift. Whyn'tcha wake me, huh?"

She mumbled a reply, her face hot and her hands constantly at her mouth; she had the urge to clamp down hard with her teeth, to keep from shrieking.

She continued to mumble, punched-out a hurried breakfast, and summarily ushered him off to his expressway.

Then she sank into a chair and had a good, deep cry.

Later, when she was certain she had control of herself, she got out the pamphlet again.

This time there was no mistaking the annoyance in the pamphlet's voice.

"You failed again. I can tell from your emanations. Very seldom does anyone need two of the methods provided by our Kits . . . you are the first one in nearly eight thousand Kits that has needed all three. We hope you are proud of yourself."

"His dirty socks," she began, "I had to get them out. I just couldn't stand the thought . . ."

"I do not wish apologies. I want attention! The third method is very simple—even a dunce—"

"There's no need to get nasty about it!" she interrupted.

"—even a *dunce* cannot fail with it," the booklet plowed on ruthlessly. "Take out the last article contained

in the Kit. The heart-globe. Do *not* agitate it as it is a
sympathetic stimulator of the heartbeat—"

Then the sound came to Madge, and the knowledge
that someone was near. Listening. She flipped the pamphlet closed, but it was too late.

Much too late.

Carl stood at the door. He showed his decaying teeth
in a brown smile without humor. "I came back," he said.
"Felt so damn tired 'n beat I just couldn't go to work . . ."

She fluttered a little. She could feel the tiny muscles
jumping all through her body. Muscles she had never
known she had.

"So that's what's been goin' on, huh Madge? I shoulda
guessed you'd get up the gut one day soon. I'll haveta
think back an' see if I can figger out what this Kit included. It'll be fun. My three was real wowzers, y'know."

She stared at him, uncomprehending. Had he found her
Kit, and had she not noticed?

"I rekcanize the pamphlet," he explained with a wave
of his meaty hand. "I sent for one of them things over
three months ago." His voice altered with incredible swiftness. Now casual and defacing, now harsh and bitter as
sump water. "But how'n a hell could I of used it around
someone like you . . . you'd of noticed the first lousy little
trap that I'd'a set . . . you'd of vacuumed an' swept an'
pried an' found it.

"I know you've hated me—but Gawd A'mighty, how
I've hated *you!* You straighten an' pick an' fuss till . . ." he
summed it all up, and ended it all, eleven years of it,
". . . till a guy can't even come home an' enjoy a belch!"

He smiled again . . . this time with dirty mirth. "Your
goddam floor's gonna get filthy today, Madge." He drew
out the long, shiny knife. "Had one of the guys in Steel
Molding make this for me . . . a *real* do-it-yourself."

Then there was pain and a feeling of incompleteness
and she saw the blood begin to drip on the rug that she
had kept so immaculate. A great deal of blood, a sea of
blood, so much blood.

Madge Rubichek had been a methodical woman . . .

So she could not check the dying statement that came
bubbling to her lips:

"There's . . . a . . . double . . . money . . . back . . ."

His voice came from far away. "I know," he said.

And in the electronically-keyed mechfiles of the Guatemalan Patent Authority, deep in the heart-banks, three assigned designates were cancelled out. Three patents drawn on a firm called simply DoMur Products, Inc.

A firm that had only a few seconds before filed bankruptcy proceedings with the Midwestern Commercial Amalgum. A firm called simply DoMur Products, Inc.

A firm that had unfortunately operated on a very, very narrow margin of profit.

Simply put, an adventure. A fable of futurity. A pastiche of men in conflict, in another time, another place, where the strength of the inner man counts for more than the bone and muscle and cartilage of the outer man. A swashbuckler and a fantasy, perhaps, but in the final analysis, when all the geegaws, foofaraws and flummery are cleared away, don't we all fight our own particular, contemporary, pressing problems in a kind of half-world of thought and phantasmagoric perception like

the silver corridor

"We can't be responsible for death or disfigurement, you know," reminded the duelsmaster.

He toyed with the company emblem on his ceremonial robe absently, awaiting Marmorth's answer. Behind him, across the onyx and crystal expanse of the reception chamber, the gaping maw of the silver corridor opened into blackness.

"Yes, yes, I know all that," snapped Marmorth impatiently. "Has Krane entered his end?" he asked, casting a glance at the dilation-segment leading to the adjoining preparation room. There was fear and apprehension in the look, only thinly hidden.

"Not quite yet," the duelsmaster told him. "By now he has signed the release, and they are briefing him, as I'm about to brief you, if you'll kindly sign yours." He indicated the printed form in the built-in frame and the stylus on the desk.

Marmorth licked his lips, grumbled briefly, and flourished the stylus on the blank line. The duelsmaster glanced quickly at the signature, then pressed the stud on the desk top. The blank slipped out of sight inside the desk. He carefully took the stylus from Marmorth's unfeeling fingers, placed it in its holder. They waited patiently for a minute. A soft clucking came up through a slot at the side of the desk, and a second later a punched plastic plate dropped into a trough beneath it.

"This is your variation-range card," explained the duelsmaster, lifting the plate from the basket. "With this we can gauge the extent of your imagination, set up the illusions, send you through the corridor at your own mental pace."

"I understand perfectly, Duelsman," snapped Marmorth. "Do you mind getting me in there! I'm freezing in this breechclout!"

"Mr. Marmorth, I realize this is annoying, but we are required both by statute of law and rule of the company to explain thoroughly the entire sequence, before entrance." He stood up behind the desk, reached into a cabinet that dilated at the approach of his hand.

"Here," he said, handing Marmorth a wraparound, "put this on till we've finished here."

Marmorth let breath whistle between his teeth in irritation, but donned the robe and sat back down in front of the desk. Marmorth was a man of medium height, hair graying slightly at the temples and forelock, a middle-aged stomach bulge. He had dark, not-quite-piercing eyes, and straight plain features. An undistinguished man at first glance, yet one who had a definite touch of authority and determination about him.

"As you know—" began the duelsmaster.

"Yes, yes, confound it! *I know, I know!* Why must you people prolong the agony of this thing?" Marmorth cut him off, rising again.

"Mr. Marmorth," resumed the duelsmaster patiently but doggedly, "if you don't settle yourself, we will call this affair off. Do you understand?"

Marmorth chuckled ruefully, deep in his throat. "After the tolls Krane and I laid out? You won't cancel."

"We will if you aren't prepared for combat. It's for your own survival, Mr. Marmorth. Now, if you'll be silent a minute, I'll brief you and you can enter the corridor."

Marmorth waved his hand negligently, grudging the duelsman his explanation. He stared in boredom at the high crystal ceiling of the reception chamber.

"The corridor, *as you know,*" went on the duelsman, adding the last phrase with sarcasm, "is a super-sensitive receptor. When you enter it, a billion scanning elements pick up your thoughts, down to the very subconscious, filter them through the banks, correlating them with your variation-range card, and feed back illusions. These illusions are matched with those of your opponent, as checked with *his* variation-range card. The illusion is always the same for both of you.

"Since you are in the field of the corridor, these are substantial illusions, and they affect you as though they were real. In other words, to illustrate the extreme—you can die at any moment. They are not dreams, I assure you, even though they are not consciously projected. All too often combatants find an illusion so strange they feel it must be unreal. May I caution you, Mr. Marmorth, that is the quickest way to lose an affair. Take everything you see at face value. *It is real!*"

He paused for a moment, wiping his forehead. He had begun to perspire freely. Marmorth wondered at this, but remained silent.

"Your handicap," the duelsmaster resumed, "is that when an illusion is formed from a larger segment of your opponent's imagination than from yours, he will be more familiar with it, and will be better able to use it against you. The same holds true for you, of course.

"The illusions will strengthen for the combatant who is dominating. In other words, if Krane's outlook is firmer than yours, he will have a more familiar illusion. If you begin to dominate him, the illusion will change to one that is more of your making.

"Do you understand?"

Marmorth had found himself listening more intently than he had thought he would. Now he had questions.

"Aren't there any weapons we begin with? I'd always thought we could choose our dueling weapons."

The duelsmaster shook his head, "No. There will be sufficient weapons in your illusions. Anything else would be superfluous."

"How can an illusion kill me?"

"You are in the corridor's field. Through a process of— well, actually, Mr. Marmorth, that is a company secret, and I doubt if it could be explained in lay terms so that you would know any more now than you did before. Just accept that the corridor converts your thought-impressions into tangibles."

"How long will we be in there?"

"Time is subjective in the corridor. You may be there

for an hour or a month or a year. Out here the time will seem as an instant. You will go in, both of you; then, a moment later—one of you will come out."

Marmorth licked his lips again. "Have there been duels where a statemate was reached—where both combatants came back?" He was nervous, and the question trembled out.

"We've never had one that I can recall," answered the duelsmaster simply.

"Oh," said Marmorth quietly, looking down at his hands.

"Are you ready now?" asked the duelsman.

Marmorth nodded silently. He slipped out of the wrap-around and laid it across the back of the chair. Together they walked toward the silver corridor. "Remember," said the duelsmaster, "the combatant who has the strongest convictions will win. That is a constant, and your only real weapon!"

The duelsmaster stepped to the end of the corridor and passed his hand across an area of wall next to its opening.

A light above the opening flashed twice, and he said, "I've signalled the duelsman on the other side. Krane has entered the corridor."

The duelsmaster slipped the variation-range card into a slot in the blank wall, then indicated Marmorth should step into the corridor.

The duelist stepped forward, smoothing the short breechclout against his thighs as he walked.

He took one step, two, three. The perfectly round mouth of the silver corridor gaped before him, black and impenetrable.

He stepped forward once more. His bare foot touched the edge of the metal, and he drew back hesitantly. He looked back over his shoulder at the duelsman. "Couldn't I—"

"Step in, Mr. Marmorth," said the duelsmaster firmly. There was a granite tone in his voice.

Marmorth walked forward into the darkness. It closed over his head and seeped behind his eyes. He felt nothing! Marmorth blinked . . .

Twice. The first time he saw the throne room and the tier-mounted pages, long-stemmed trumpets at their sides.

He saw the assembled nobles bowing low before him, their ermine capes sweeping the floor. The floor was a rich, inlaid mosaic, the walls dripped color and rich tapestry, the ceiling was high-arched and studded with crystal chandeliers.

The second time he opened them, hoping his senses had cleared, he saw precisely the same thing. Then he saw Krane—*High Lord* Krane, he somehow knew—in the front ranks.

The garb was different—a tight suit of chain-mail in blued-steel, ornamental decorations across the breastplate, a ruby-hilted sword in a scabbard at the waist, full, flowing cape of blood-red velvet—but the face was no different from the one Marmorth had seen in the Council Chamber, before they had agreed to duel.

The face was thin: a V that swept past a high, white forehead and thick, black brows, past the high cheekbones and needle-thin nose, down to the slash mouth and pointed black beard. A study in coal and chalk.

The man's hair had been swept back to form a tight knot at the base of his skull. It was the knot of the triumphant warrior.

Marmorth's blood churned at the sight of the despised Krane! If he hadn't challenged Marmorth's Theorem in the Council Chamber, with his insufferable slanders, neither of them would be here.

Here!

Marmorth stiffened. He sat more erect. The word swept away his momentary forgetfulness: this was the silver corridor. This was illusion. They were dueling—now, at this instant! He had to kill Krane.

But whose illusion was this? His own, or the dark-bearded scoundrel's before him? It might be suicide to attempt killing Krane in his own illusion. He would have to wait a bit and gauge what the situation represented in his own mind.

Whatever it was, he seemed to be of higher rank than Krane, who bowed before him.

Almost magically, before he realized the words were emerging from his mouth, he heard himself saying, "Lord Krane, rise!"

The younger man stood up, and the other nobles followed suit, the precedent having been set. By choosing

Krane to rise first, Marmorth the King had chosen whom he wanted to speak first in the Star Chamber.

"May it please Your Illustriousness," boomed Krane, extending his arms in salute, "I have a disposition of the prisoners from Quorth. I should beg Your Eminence's verdict on my proposal."

He bowed his head and awaited Marmorth's reply.

Had there been a tone of mockery in the man's voice? Marmorth could not be sure. But he did know, now, that it was his own illusion. If Krane was coming to *him* for disposition, then he must be in the ascendant in this creation.

"What is your proposal, High Lord Krane?" asked Marmorth.

Krane took a step forward, bringing him to the bottom of the dais upon which Marmorth's throne rested.

"These *things* are of a totally alien culture, Your Highness," began Krane. "How can we, as humans, even tolerate their existence in our way of life? The very sight of them makes the gorge rise! They are evil-smelling and accursedly-formed! They must all be destroyed, Your Highness! We must ignore the guileful offers of a prisoner-for-prisoner exchange! We will have our fleet in Quorth City within months; then we can rescue our own captured without submitting to the demands of four monsters! In the meantime, why feed these beasts of another world?

"I say, destroy them! Launch all-out attack now! Rescue our people from the alien's slave camps on Quorth and Fetsa!"

He had been speaking smoothly and forcefully. The nods of assent and agreement from the assembled nobles made Marmorth wary. A complete knowledge of the Quorth-Human war was in his mind, and the plan of Krane sounded clear and fine. Yet, superimposed over it, was his knowledge that this was all merely illusion and that somewhere in the illusion might be a chink in which his errors could lodge. The plan sounded good, but . . .

"No, Krane!" he decided, thinking quickly. "This would be what the aliens want! They *want* us to destroy our prisoners. That would whip their people at home into such a frenzy of patriotism—we would be engulfed in a month!

"We will consider the alien proposal of prisoner-for-prisoner exchange."

The rumbles from the massed nobles rose into the cavern of the Star Chamber. There was unrest here.

He had to demonstrate that he was right. "Let them bring in the chain of aliens!" he commanded, clapping his hands. A page went out swiftly.

While the hall waited, Marmorth concentrated fiercely; had he made the proper decision? There seemed to be a correlation between Krane's challenging of his Theorem of Government in the Council—back in the world outside the corridor—and this proposal he had just defeated.

There *was* a correlation! He saw it suddenly!

Both his proposal of the Theorem in the Council and his decision here in the illusion had been based on his personal concept of government. Krane's refutation out there and his proposal here were the opposite. Once again they had clashed.

And this time Marmorth had won!

But had he?

Even as he let the thought filter, the chained aliens were dragged between the massed nobles and cast on their triple-jointed knees before Marmorth's dais. "Here are the loathesome beings!" cried Krane, flinging his arms high and apart.

It had been a grandstand gesture, and the frog-faced, many-footed beings on the Star Chamber's floor realized it.

Suddenly, almost as though they were made of paper, the chains that had joined the aliens snapped, and they leaped on the nobles.

Marmorth caught the smile on Krane's lips. *He* had been behind this; probably had the chains severed in the corridor outside by some henchman!

Without thinking, Marmorth was off his throne and down the stepped dais, his sword free from its scabbard and arcing viciously.

A hideously warted alien face rose before him and he thrust with all his might! The blade pierced between the double-lidded eyes, and thick ochre blood spurted across his tunic. He yanked the blade free, kicking the dead but still quivering alien from its length. He leaped, howling a familiar battle-cry.

Even as he leaped, he saw Krane's slash-mouthed smile, and the Lord's sword swinging toward him!

So it *hadn't* been his illusion! It had been Krane's! He hadn't chosen the proper course. Krane's belief at the moment was stronger than his own.

He fended off a double-handed smash from the black-bearded noble, and fell back. They parried and countered, thrust and slashed all around the dais. The other nobles were too deeply involved fighting off the screaming aliens to witness this battle between their King and his Lord.

Krane beat Marmorth back, back!

Why did I choose as I did? Marmorth wailed mentally, berating himself.

Suddenly he slipped, toppling backwards onto the steps. The sword flew from his hand as it cracked against the edge of a step. He saw Krane bearing down on him, the sword double-fisted as his opponent raised it like a stake above his head.

In desperation, Marmorth summoned up all his belief. "*It* was *the right decision!*" screamed Marmorth with the conviction of a man about to die. He saw the sword plunge toward his breast as ...

He gathered the light about him, sweeping his hands through the dripping colors, making them shift and flow. He saw the figure of Krane, standing haughtily in the bank of yellow, and he gathered the blue to himself in a coruscating ball.

Fearsomely he bellowed his challenge, "This is *my* illusion, Krane! Watch as I kill you!"

He balled the blue in his hand and sent it flying, dripping sparks and color as it shot toward the black-bearded man.

They both stood tall and spraddle-legged in the immensity of they knew-not-where. The colors dripped from the air, making weird patterns as they mixed.

The blue ball struck in front of Krane and exploded, cascading a rich flood of chromatic brilliance into the air. Krane laughed at the failure.

He gathered the black to him, wadding it in strong and supple fingers. He wound up, almost as though it were a sport, and flung the wadded black at Marmorth.

The older man knew he had not yet built enough belief

to withstand this onslaught. If the black enfolded him he would die in the never-ending limbo of nothingness.

He thrust hands up before his face to stop the onrush of the black, but it struck him and he fell, clutching feebly at a washy stringer of white.

He fell into the black as it billowed up to surround him.

This was not his illusion! It could not be, for he was vanquished! Yet he was not dead, as he had felt sure he would be. He lay there, thinking.

He remembered all the effort he had put in on the Political Theorem. The Theorem he had proposed in the Council. It had represented years of work—the culmination of all his adult thought and effort; and, he had to admit, the Theorem was soundly based on his own view of the Universe.

Then the presumptuous Krane had offended him by restating the Theorem.

Krane had, of course, twisted it to his own evil and malicious ends—basing it anew on *his* conception of the All.

There had been a verbal battle. There had been the accusations, the clanging of the electric gavel, the remonstrances of the Compjudge, the shocked expressions of the other Councillors! Till finally Marmorth had been goaded by the younger man into the duel. Into the silver corridor.

Only one of them would emerge. The one who did would force his own version of the Theorem on the Council. To be accepted, and used as a basis for future decisions and policy. Each Theorem—Marmorth's monumental original, and Krane's malformed copy—was all-inclusive.

It all revolved, then, around whose view of the Universe, whose Theorem, was the right one. And it was inconceivable to Marmorth that Krane could be correct.

Marmorth struck out at the black! *Mine, mine, mine!* he shouted soundlessly. He lashed into the nothingness. *My Theorem is the proper one! It is true! Krane's is based on deceit!*

Then he saw the stringer of white in his hand. So this was Krane in the ascendant, was it? Now came the moment of retaliation!

He whipped the stringer around his head, swaying as

he was, there in the depthless black. The stringer thickened. He cupped it to him, washing it with his hands, strengthening it, shaping and molding it.

In a moment it had grown. In a moment more the white had burst forth like a rope blossom and flooded all. Revealing Krane standing there, in his breechclout, massaging the pale pink between his fingers.

"Mine, Krane, *mine!*" he screamed, flinging the white!

Krane blanched and tried to duck. The white came on like a sliver of Forever, streaking and burning as it rode currents that did not exist. Then the light shattered, blazed into thousands of spitting fragments. As Marmorth realized they had nullified each other again, that the illusion was dissolving around them, he heard Krane bellow, as loud as Marmorth himself, had, "Mine, Marmorth, *mine!*"

The colors ran. They flowed, they merged, they sucked at his body, while he . . .

Shrank up against the glass wall next to Krane. They both stared in fascinated horror as the huge, ichor-dripping spider-thing advanced on them, mandibles clicking.

"My God in Heaven!" Marmorth heard Krane bellow. "What is it?" Krane scrabbled at the glass wall behind him, trying to get out. They were trapped.

The glass walls circled them. They were trapped with the spider-thing and each other, trapped in the tiny tomb!

Marmouth was petrified. He could not move or speak— he could hardly sense anything but terror. Spiders were his greatest personal fear. He found his legs were quivering at the knees, though he had not sensed it a moment before. The very sight of the hairy beasts had always sent shudders through him. Now he knew this was an illusion—his illusion. *He* was in the ascendant!

But how hideously in the ascendant. He wondered, almost hysterically, if he could control the illusion—use it against Krane.

The spider-thing advanced on them, the soft plush pads of its hundred feet leaving dampness where it stepped.

Krane fell to his knees, moaning and scratching at the glass floor. "Out, out, out, out . . ." he mumbled, froth dripping from his lips.

Marmorth realized this was his chance. This fear was a

product of his own mind; he had lived with it all his life.
He knew it more familiarly than Krane—he could not
cancel it, certainly, but he could utilize it more easily
than the other.

Here was where he would kill Krane. He pulled himself
tightly to the wall, sweating palms flat to the glass, the
valley of his backbone against the cool surface. "I'm right!
The Theorem as I stated it i-is c-correct!" He said it tri-
umphantly, though the note of terror quivered undisguised in his voice.

The spider-thing paused in its march, swung its clicking,
ghastly head about as though confused, and altered direction by an inch. Away from Marmorth. It descended on
Krane.

The black-bearded man looked up, saw it coming toward
him, heard Marmorth's words. Even on the floor, half-
sunk in shock, he shouted, pounding his fists against the
floor of glass, "Wrong, wrong, wrong! You're wrong; I
can prove *my* Theorem is correct! The basic formation of
the Judiciary should be planned in an ever-decreasing
system of—"

Marmorth didn't even listen. He knew it was drivel! He
knew the man was wrong! But the spider-thing had stopped
once more. Now it paused between the two of them, its
bulk shivering as though caught in a draft.

Krane saw the hesitation on the monster's part, and
rose, the old confidence and impudence regained. He
wiped his balled fists across his eyes, clearing them of
tears. He continued speaking, steadily, in the voice of a
fanatic. The man just could *not* recognize that he was
wrong.

"You're insane, man!" Marmorth interjected, waving his
hands with fervor. "The economy must be balanced by a
code of fair practices with a guild system blocking efforts
on the part of the Genres to rise into the control of the
main weath!" He went on and on, outlining the original
—the only true—Theorem.

Krane, too, shouted and gesticulated, both of them suddenly oblivious to the monstrous, black spider-thing
which had stopped completely between them, vacillating.

When Marmorth stopped for an instant to regain his
breath, the beast would twist its neckless head toward
him. Marmorth would then speed up his speech, spewing

out detail upon detail, and the beast would sink back into uncertainty.

It was obviously a battle of belief. Whichever combatant had more conviction—that one would win.

They stood and shouted, screamed, outlined, explained and delineated for what seemed hours. Finally, as though in exasperation, the spider-thing began to turn. They both watched it, their mouths working, words pouring forth in twin streams of absolute, sincere belief.

They watched while . . .

The starships fired at each other mercilessly. Blast after blast exploded soundlessly into the vault of space. Marmorth found his fingers twisted in the epaulette at his right shoulder.

As he watched Krane's *Magnificent*-class destroyer wheel in the control-room screens, a half-naked, blood-soaked and perspiring crewman burst into the cabin's entrance-well.

"Captain, Captain, sir!" he implored.

Marmorth looked over the plastic rail, down into the well.

"What?" he snapped with brittleness.

"Cap'n, the port side is riddled! We're losing pressure from thirteen compartments. The reclamation mile is completely lost! The engineers group was in one of the compartments along that mile, Cap'n! They're all bloated and blue and dead in there! We can see them floating around without any . . ."

"Get the Hell out of here!" Marmorth snapped, lifting a spacetant from his chart-board and flinging it with all his strength at the crewman. The man ducked and the spacetant bounced off the bulkhead, snapping pieces from its intricate bulk.

"You maniac!" the man yowled, leaping back out of the well, through the exit port, as Marmorth reached for another missile.

Marmorth shut his eyes tight, blanking out the shuddering ship, space, the screens, everything.

"Right, right, right, right, right! I'm right!" he shouted, lifting clenched fists.

The explosion came in two parts, as though two torpedoes had been struck almost simultaneously. The ship rocked and heeled. Bits of metal sheared through the outer bulkheads, crashed against the opposite wall.

As the lights went dead, and the screams drove into his brain, Marmorth shouted his credo once more, with all the force of his conviction, with all the power of his lungs, with all the strength in his gasping body.

"I'm right! May God strike me dead if I'm not right! I know I'm right, I made an inexhaustible . . .

"Check!" he finished, opening his eyes and looking back down at the chessboard. The pieces had, happily, not moved. He still had Krane blocked off.

"I say check," he repeated, smiling, steepling his fingers. Krane's black-bearded face broke into a wry grimace.

"Most clever, my dear Marmorth," he congratulated the other with sarcasm. "You have forced me to touch a bishop."

Marmorth watched as Krane, with trembling fingers, reached down to the jet bishop. It was carved from stone, carved with such care and intricacy that its edges were precisely as they had been desired by the master craftsman. They were razor sharp.

The pieces were all cut the same. Both the blanched alabaster pieces before Marmorth, and the ebony-stone players under Krane's hand. The game had been constructed for men who played more than a "gentleman's game." There was death in each move.

Marmorth knew he was in the ascendant. Each of them had had two illusions—that remembrance was sharp— and this was Marmorth's. How did he know? The older man looked down at the intricately-carved chess pieces. He was white, Krane was black. As clear as it could be.

"Uh, have you moved?" Marmorth inquired, his voice adrip with casualness. He knew the other had not yet touched his players. "I believe you still lie in check," he reminded.

He thought he heard a muted, "Damn you!" under Krane's breath, but could not be certain.

Slowly Krane touched the player, carefully sliding the fingers of his hand across the razor-thin, razor-sharp facets. The piece almost slid from his grasp, so loosely was he holding it, but the move was made in an instant.

Marmorth cursed mentally. Krane had calculated beautifully! Not only was his king blocked out from Marmorth's rook—Marmorth's check-piece—but in another two moves (so clearly obvious, as Krane had desired it) his own queen would be in danger. In his mind he could hear Krane savoring the words: *"Garde! I say garde, my dear Marmorth!"*

He had to move the queen out of position.

He had to touch the queen!

The most deadly piece on the board!

"No!" he gasped.

"I beg your pardon?" said Krane, the slash-mouth opening in a twisted grin.

"N-nothing, nothing!" snapped Marmorth. He concentrated.

There was little chance he could maneuver that thousand-edged queen without bleeding to death for his trouble. Lord! It was an insoluble, a double-edged, dilemma. If he did not move, Krane would win. If he won, it was obvious that Marmorth would die. He had seen the deadly dirk's hilt protruding slightly from Krane's cummerbund when the other had sat down. If he *did* move, he would bleed to death before Krane's taunting eyes.

You shall never have that pleasure! he thought, the bitter determination of a man who will not be defeated rising in him.

He approached the queen, with hand, with eye.

The base was faceted, like a diamond. Each facet ended in a cutting edge so sensitive he knew it would sever the finger that touched it. The shape of the upper segments was involved, gorgeously-made. A woman, arms raised above her head, stretching in tension. Beautiful—and untouchable.

Then the thought struck him: *Is this the only move?*

Deep within his mind he calculated. He could not possibly recognize the levels on which his intellect was working. In with his chess theory, in with his mental agility, in with his desire to win, his Theorem re-arranged itself, fitting its logic to this situation. How could the Theorem be applied to the game? What other paths, through the infallible truth of the Theorem—in which he believed, now, more strongly than ever before—could he take?

Then the alternative move became clear. He could escape a rout, escape the *garde*, escape the taunting smile of Krane by moving a relatively safe knight. It was not a completely foolproof action, since the knight, too, was a razored piece of death, but he had found a way to avoid certain defeat by Krane's maneuverings.

"Ha!" the terrible smile burst upon his face. His eyes bored across to the other's. Krane turned white as Marmorth reached out, touched one piece he had been desperately hoping the older man would not consider.

Marmorth felt an uncontrollable tightening in his throat as he realized the game would go on, and on, and on and . . .

He unclenched his fist as the volcano leaped up around them.

It was more than the inside of a volcanic cone, however. The corridor was there, too. The dung-brown walls of smooth rock shivered ever so slightly, and both men knew the silver corridor was just beyond their vision. They could see it glimmering with unreality.

It was almost as though they were looking at a double exposure; an extinct volcano superimposed over the shining tube of the silver corridor.

It isn't far away, thought Marmorth. He felt, with a sudden release of nervous tension, *Someone is going to win soon.*

He stared up at the faint patch of gray sky, visible through the roundly jagged opening at the cone's top. The walls sloped down in a fluid concavity. Here and there across the rough floor of the cavern, stalagmites rose up in sharp spikes.

And there—over and through the walls of the dead formations—the corridor hung faintly. A ghostly, shivering, not-quite-real shadow, inside the substance of their illusion.

They stood and stared at each other. Each knowing they were not really in the heart of a volcano, but in a metal corridor. Each knowing they could die as easily by this illusion as they could at each other's hands. Each asking the same questions.

Was this the end? Were there a limited number of illusions to each affair? A set pattern to each duel? Who had won? Could there *be* a winner?

They stared at each other, across the dusky interior of the extinct volcano.

"I'm right," said Krane, hesitantly.

"You're wrong," answered Marmorth quickly. *"I'm* the one who's right!"

In a moment they were at it again, each screaming till his lungs were raw with the effort, and red patches had appeared in their cheeks. They paused for an instant, gathering air for another tirade, Krane looking about him for a weapon.

They were both as they had begun. Naked save the breechclouts which clung to their buttocks.

They resumed their shouting, the sound reverberating hollowly in the dim interior of the volcano. The sounds hit them, bounced across the stone walls, reverberated again. The fury had been built to a peak and pitch they both knew could not be exceeded. They had strained every last vestige of belief and conviction in their minds.

As Marmorth realized he was at the pinnacle of his belief, he saw the same conviction come over Krane's face. He knew that from here on in, it would be a physical thing, with both of them stalemated in illusory power.

Then the woman-thing appeared.

She plopped into being between them. She wasn't human. There was no question about that. Marmorth took a halting step backward. Krane remained rooted, though his pale face had blanched an even more deadly shade. A strangled, "My God, what *is* it?" slipped past Marmorth's lips.

It was less than human, yet more than mortal; it was a travesty of a human being. A mad nightmare of a vision! Like some fearsome god of an ancient cult, it paused with long legs apart, hands on hips.

The woman's body was lush. Full, high breasts, trim stomach, exciting legs. Gorgeously proportioned and seductive, the torso and legs, the chest and arms, were normal—even exaggeratedly normal.

But there all resemblance to a woman ceased.

The head was a lizard-like thing, with elongated snout, wattles, huge glowing eyes set atop the skull. Looking out through flesh-sockets thick and deep—little hummocks atop the face—the eyes were small, crimson and cruel.

The nose was almost nonexistent. Two breather-spaces pulsed, one on either side of a small rise in the yellowed, pocked flesh of the head.

The mouth was a wide, gaping, and triangular orifice, with triple rows of shark teeth in the upper and lower jaws. The woman-thing looked like a gorgeous female—with the weirdly altered head of a crocodile.

The ebony, leathery, bat's wings rising from the shoulder blades—quivering—completed the frightening picture.

Wisps of smoky, filmy garments were draped over the woman-thing's shoulders, around her waist. She stood absolutely unmoving.

Then she spoke to them.

It was not mental. It actually sounded, but not from the body before them. They knew it was—her?—but it did not come from her at all. The fearful mouth remained almost shut, propped slightly open on the sharp tiers of teeth.

The voice issued from the walls, from the tips of the stalactites, from the high, arching roof of the volcano; it boomed from the rocky floor—it even floated down the length of the infinitely-stretching corridor.

The voice spoke in thunder, yet softly.

Well, Gentlemen?

Krane stared for a second at the woman-thing; then he looked about wildly, trying to find the source of the voice. His head swung back and forth as though it were manipulated by strings from above. "Well, *what?*" he shouted to no one.

Have you realized the truth yet?

"What truth? What are you talking about? Who is that? Is it you?" chimed in Marmorth, bathed in sudden fear.

The corridor shimmered oddly, just behind the stone walls of the volcano.

I'm a voice, Gentlemen. A voice and an illusion. Just an illusion, that's all, Gentlemen. Just an illusion from both of your minds. Made of equal portions of your mind. For you are each as strong as the other.

There was a pause. Marmorth could not speak. Then:

But tell me, have you realized what you should have known before you were foolish enough to enter the corridor?

Krane looked at Marmorth with suspicion. For the first time it seemed to occur to him that perhaps this was a trick on the other's part. Marmorth, recognizing the glance, shrugged his shoulders eloquently.

He found his voice. "No! Tell us, then! *What* should we have known?"

The only real answer as to who is right: which Theorem is the correct one!

"Tell me, tell me!" they shouted, almost together.

There was silence for a moment. The woman-thing ran a scarlet-tipped hand across the hideous lizard snout, as though searching for a way to phrase what was coming. Then the single word sounded in the heart of the volcano.

Neither.

Krane and Marmorth stared past the woman-thing, stared at each other in confusion. "N-neither?" shouted Marmorth incredulously. "Are you mad? Of course one of us is right! Me!" He was shaking fists at the gruesome being before him. Illusion, perhaps; but an illusion that was goading him.

"Prove it! Prove it!" screamed Krane, stepping forward, flat-footedly, as though seeking to strike the woman-thing.

Then the voice gave them the solution and the proof that neither could contest, for both knew it to be true on a level that defied mere conviction.

You are both egomaniacs. You could not possibly be convinced of the other's viewpoint. Not in a hundred million years. Any message dies between you. You are both too tightly ensnared in yourselves!

The woman-thing suddenly began to shiver. She became indistinct, and there were many shadow-forms of her, surrounding her body like halos. Abruptly, she disappeared from between them—leaving them alone in the quickening darkness of the volcano's throat.

Alone. Staring at each other with dawning comprehension, dawning belief.

They both realized it at the same moment. They both had the conviction of their cause, yet they both knew the woman-thing had been right.

"Krane," said Marmorth, starting toward the black-bearded man, "she's right, you know. Perhaps we can get together and figure . . ."

The other had started toward the older man as he had spoken.

"Yes, perhaps there's something in what you say. Perhaps there's a . . ."

At the instant they both realized it—the instant each considered the other's viewpoint—the illusion barriers shattered, of course, and the red-hot lava poured in on them, engulfing both men completely in a blistering inferno.

What kind of a culture are we breeding around us? A society in which everyone tries to be average, right on the norm, the common denominator, the median, the great leveler. College kids demonstrating a callow conservativism that urges them not to stick their heads above the crowd, not to be noticed. Political candidates so bland they must of necessity be faceless to gain identification with their equally faceless constituents. A sameness in thinking, in demeanor, in dress, in goals, in desires. More than the obvious threats of cobalt bombs, World Communism, famine, plague, pestilence or the singing of The Everly Brothers, I fear for the safety of my country and its people from this creeping paralysis of the ego. I have tried to say something about it in

all the sounds of fear

"Give me some light!"

Cry: tormented, half-moan half-chant, cast out against a whispering darkness; a man wound in white, arms upflung to roistering shadows, sooty sockets where eyes had been, pleading, demanding, anger and hopelessness, anguish from the soul into the world. He stumbled, a step, two, faltering, weak, the man returned to the child, trying to find some exit from the washing sea of darkness in which he trembled.

"Give me some light!"

Around him a Greek chorus of sussurating voices; plucking at his garments he staggered toward an intimation of sound, a resting-place, a goal. The man in pain, the figure of *all* pain, all desperation, and nowhere in that circle of painful light was there release from his torment. Sandaled feet stepping, each one above an abyss, no hope and no safety; what can it mean to be so eternally blind?

Again, "Give me some light!"

The last tortured ripping of the words from a throat raw with the hopelessness of salvation. Then the man sank to the shadows that moved in on him. The face half-hidden in chiaroscuro, sharp black, blanched white, down

61

and down into the greyness about his feet, the circle of
blazing white light pinpointing him, a creature impaled on
a pin of brilliance, till closing, closing, closing it swallowed
him, all gone to black, darkness within and without, black
even deeper, nothing, finis, end; silence.

Richard Becker, Oedipus, had played his first rôle.
Twenty-four years later, he would play it again, as his
last. But before that final performance's curtain could be
rung, twenty-four years of greatness would have to strut
across stages of life and theatre and emotion.

Time: passing.

When they had decided to cast the paranoid beggar
in "Sweet Miracles," Richard Becker had gone to the Salvation Army retail store, and bought a set of rags that
even the sanctimonious charity-workers staffing the shop
had tried to throw out as unsalable and foul. He bought a
pair of cracked and soleless shoes that were a size too
large. He bought a hat that had seen so many autumns of
rain its brim had bowed and withered under the onslaught.
He bought a no-color vest from a suit long since destroyed, and a pair of pants whose seat sagged raggedly,
and a shirt with three buttons gone, and a jacket that
seemed to typify every derelict who had ever cadged an
hour's sleep in an alley.

He bought these things over the protests of the kindly,
white-haired women who were *doing their bit for charity*, and he asked if he might step into the toilet for a
few moments to try them on; and when he emerged, his
good tweed jacket and dark slacks over his arm, he was
another man entirely. As though magically, the coarse
stubble (that may have been there when he came into
the store, but who was too nice-looking a young man to
go around unshaved) had sprouted on his sagging jowls.
The hair had grown limp and off-grey under the squashed
hat. The face was lined and planed with the depravities
and deprivations of a lifetime lived in gutters and saloons.
The hands were caked with filth, the eyes lusterless and
devoid of personality, the body grotesquely slumped by
the burden of mere existence. This old man, this skid
from the Bowery, how had he gotten into the toilet, and
where was the nice young man who had gone in wearing
that jacket and those slacks? Had this *creature* somehow

overpowered him (what foul weapon had this feeble old man used to subdue a vital, strong youth like that)? The white-haired Good Women of Charity were frozen with distress as they imagined the strong-faced, attractive youth, lying in the bathroom, his skull crushed by a length of pipe.

The old bum extended the jacket, the pants, and the rest of the clothing the young man had been wearing, and in a voice that was thirty years younger than the body from which it spoke, he explained, "I won't be needing these, ladies. Sell them to someone who can make good use of them." The voice of the young man, from this husk.

And he paid for the rags he wore. They watched him as he limped and rolled through the front door, into the filthy streets, another tramp gone to join the tide of lost souls that would inevitably become a stream and a river and an ocean of wastrels, washing finally into a drunk tank, or a doorway, or a park bench.

Richard Becker spent six weeks living on the Bowery; in fleabags, abandoned warehouses, cellars, gutters, and on tenement rooftops, he shared and wallowed in the nature and filth and degradation of the empty men of his times.

For six weeks he *was* a tramp, a thoroughly washed-out hopeless rumdum, with rheumy eyes and palsied wrists and a weak bladder.

One by one the weeks mounted to six, and on the first day of casting for "Sweet Miracles," the Monday of the seventh week, Richard Becker arrived at the Royale Theatre, where he auditioned for the part in the clothes he had worn for the past six weeks.

The play ran for five hundred and eighteen performances, and Richard Becker won the Drama Critics Circle Award as the finest male performer of the year. He also won the Circle Award as the most promising newcomer of the year.

He was twenty-two years old at the time.

The following season, after "Sweet Miracles" had gone on the road, Richard Becker was apprised, through the pages of *Variety*, that John Foresman & T. H. Searle were about to begin casting for "House of Infidels," the new script by Odets, his first in many years. Through friends in the Foresman & Searle offices, he obtained a copy of the script, and selected a part he considered massive in its potentialities.

The role of an introspective and tormented artist, depressed by the level of commercialism to which his work had sunk, resolved to regain an innocence of childhood or nature he had lost, by working with his hands in a foundry.

When the first night critics called Richard Becker's conception of Tresk, the artist, "a pinnacle of thespic intuition" and noted, "His authority in the part led members of the audience to ask one another how such a sensitive actor could grasp the rough unsubtle life of a foundryworker," they had no idea that Richard Becker had worked for nearly two months in a steel stamping plant and foundry in Pittsburgh. But the makeup man on "House of Infidels" suspected Richard Becker had once been in a terrible fire, for his hands were marked by the ravages of great heat.

After two successes, two conquests of Broadway, two characterizations that were immediately ranked with the most brilliant Schubert Alley had ever witnessed, Richard Becker's reputation began to build a legend.

The Man Who IS *The "Method,"* they called him, in perceptive articles and interviews. Lee Strassberg of the Actor's Studio, when questioned, remarked that Becker had never been a student, but had the occasion arisen, he might well have paid *him* to attend. In any event, Richard Becker's command of the Stanislavski theory of total immersion in a part became a working example of the validity of the concept. No mere scratcher and stammerer, Richard Becker *was* the man he pretended to be, on a stage.

Of his private life little was known, for he let it be known that if he was to be totally convincing in a characterization, he wanted no intrusive shadow of himself to stand between the audience and the image he offered.

Hollywood's offers of stardom were refused, for as *Theatre Arts* commented in a brief feature on Richard Becker:

"The gestalt that Becker projects across a row of footlights would be dimmed and turned two-dimensional on the Hollywood screen. Becker's art is an ultimate distillation of truth and metamorphosis that requires the reality of stage production to retain its purity. It might even be noted that Richard Becker acts in *four* dimensions, as opposed to the merely craftsmanlike three of his contemporaries. Surely no one could truly argue with the fact that watching a Becker performance is almost a religious experience. We can only congratulate Richard Becker on his perceptiveness in turning down studio bids."

The years of building a backlog of definitive parts (effectively ruining them for other actors who were condemned to play them after Becker had said all there was to say) passed, as Richard Becker became, in turn, a Hamlet that cast new lights on the Freudian implications of Shakespeare . . . a fiery Southern segregationist whose wife reveals her octaroon background . . . a fast-talking salesman come to grips with futility and cowardice . . . a many-faceted Marco Polo . . . a dissolute and totally amoral pimp, driven by a loathing for women, to sell his own sister into evil . . . a ruthless politician, dying of cancer and senility . . .

And the most challenging part he had ever undertaken, the re-creation, in the play by Tennessee Williams, of the deranged religious zealot, trapped by his own warring emotions, into the hammer-murder of an innocent girl . . .

. . . when they found him, in the model's apartment off Gramercy Place, they were unable to get a coherent story of why he had done the disgusting act, for he had lapsed into a stentorian tone of Biblical fervor, pontificating about the blood of the lamb and the curse of Jezebel and the eternal fires of Perdition. The men from Homicide numbered among their ranks a rookie, fresh to the squad, who became desperately ill at the sight of the fouled walls and the crumpled form wedged into the tiny kitchenette; he became violently ill, and was taken from the apartment a few minutes before Richard Becker was led away.

The trial was a manifest sadness to all who had seen him onstage, and the jury did not even have to be sent out to agree on a verdict of insanity.

After all, whoever the fanatic was that the defense put on the stands, he was not sane, and was certainly no longer Richard Becker, the actor.

For Dr. Charles Tedrow, the patient in restraining room 16 was a constant involvement. He was unable to divorce himself from the memory of a night three years before, when he had sat in an orchestra seat at the Henry Miller Theatre, and seen Richard Becker, light and adroit, as the comical Tosspot in that season's hit comedy, "Never a Rascal".

He was unable to separate his thoughts from the shape and form of the actor who had so immersed himself in The Method that for a time, in three acts, he *was* a blundering, maundering, larcenous alcoholic with a penchant for pomegranates and (as Becker had mouthed it onstage) "barratry on the low seas!" Separate them from this weird and many-faceted creature that lived its many lives in the padded cell numbered 16.

At first, there had been reporters, who had come to interview the Good Doctor in charge of Becker's case, and to the last of these (for Dr. Tedrow had instituted restrictions on this sort of publicity) he had said, "To a man like Richard Becker, the world was very important. He was very much a man of his times; he had no real personality of his own, with the exception of that one overwhelming faculty and need to reflect the world around him. He was an actor in the purest sense of the word. The world gave him his personality, his attitudes, his reason and his façade for existence. Take those away from him, clap him up in a padded cell—as we were forced to do—and he begins to lose touch with reality."

"I understand," the reporter had inquired carefully, "that Becker is re-living his roles, one after another. Is that true, Dr. Tedrow?"

Charles Tedrow was, above all else, a compassionate man, and his fury at this remark, revealing as it did a leak in the sanitarium's security policy, was manifest. "Richard Becker is undergoing what might be called, in psychiatric terms, 'induced hallucinatory regression.' In his search for some reality, there in that room, he has fastened on the method of assuming characters' moods he had played onstage. From what I've been able to piece together from reviews of his shows, he is going back from the most recent to the next and the next and so on."

The reporter had asked more questions, more superficial and phantasmagoric assumptions, until Dr. Charles Tedrow had concluded the interview forcibly.

But even now, as he sat across from Richard Becker, in the quiet office, he knew that almost nothing the reporter had conceived, could rival what Becker had done to himself.

"Tell me, Doctor," the florid, bombastic traveling salesman who was Richard Becker asked, "what the hell's new down the line?"

"It's really very quiet, these days, Ted," the physician replied. Becker had been this way for two months now: submerged in the part of Ted Rogat, the loudmouth philandering protagonist of Chayefsky's "The Wanderer." For six months before that he had been Marco Polo, and before that the nervous, slack-jawed and incestuous son of "The Glass of Sadness."

"Hell, I remember one little chippie in, where was it, oh yeah, hell yes! It was K.C., good old K.C. Man, she was a *goodie!* You ever been to K.C., Doc? I was a drummer in nylons when I worked K.C. Jeezus, lemme tell ya—"

It was difficult to believe the man who sat on the other side of the table was an actor. He looked the part, he spoke the part, he *was* Ted Rogat, and Dr. Tedrow could catch himself from time to time contemplating the release of this total stranger who had wandered into Richard Becker's cell.

He sat and listened to the story of the flame-hipped harlot in Kansas City that Ted Rogat had picked up in an Armenian Restaurant, and seduced with promises of nylons. He listened to it, and knew that whatever else was true of Richard Becker, this creature of many faces and many lives, he was no saner than the day he had killed that girl. After eighteen months in the sanitarium, he was going back, back, back through his acting career, and re-playing the roles, but never once coming to grips with reality.

In the plight and disease of Richard Becker, Dr. Charles Tedrow saw a bit of himself, of all men, of his times and the thousand illnesses to which they were heir.

He returned Richard Becker, as well as Ted Rogat, to the security and tiny world of Room 16.

Two months later he brought him back, and spent a highly interesting three hours discussing group therapy with Herr Doktor Ernst Loebisch, credentials from the Munich Academy of Medicine and the Vienna Psychiatric Clinic. Four months after that, Dr. Tedrow got to know the surly and insipid Jackie Bishoff, juvenile delinquent and hero of "Streets of Night."

And almost a year later, to the day, Dr. Tedrow sat in his office with a bum, a derelict, a rheumy-eyed and dissipated vagabond who could only be the skid from "Sweet Miracles," Richard Becker's first triumph, twenty-four years before.

What Richard Becker might look like, without camouflage, in his own shell, Tedrow had no idea. He was, now, to all intents and purposes, the seedy old tramp with the dirt caked into the sagged folds of his face.

"Mr. Becker, I want to talk to you."

Hopelessness shined out of the old bum's eyes. There was no answer.

"Listen to me, Becker. Please listen to me, if you're in there somewhere, if you can hear me. I want you to understand what I'm about to say; it's very important."

A croak, cracked and forced, came from the bum's lips, and he mumbled, "I need'a drink, yuh go' uh drink fuh me, huh . . ."

Tedrow leaned across, his hand shaking as he took the old bum's chin in his palm, and held it fixed, staring into this stranger's eyes. "Now listen to me, Becker. You've got to hear me. I've gone through the files, and as far as I can tell, this was the first part you ever played. I don't know what will happen! I don't know what form this syndrome will take after you've used up all your other lives. But if you can hear me, you've got to understand that you may be approaching a critical period in your— in your life."

The old bum licked cracked lips.

"Listen! I'm here, I want to help you, I want to *do* something for you, Becker. If you'll come out for an instant, just a second, we can establish contact. It's got to be now or—"

He left it hanging. He had no way of knowing *if-*

what. And as he lapsed into silence, as he released the bum's chin, a strange alteration of facial muscles began, and the derelict's countenance shifted, subtly ran like hot lead, and for a second he saw a face he recognized. From the eyes that were no longer red-rimmed and bloodshot, Dr. Charles Tedrow saw intelligence peering out.

"It sounds like fear, Doctor," Richard Becker said.

And, "Goodbye, once more."

Then the light died, the face shifted once again, and the physician was staring once more at the empty face of a gutter-bred derelict.

He sent the old man back to Room 16. Later that day, he had one of the male nurses take in an 89¢ bottle of muscatel.

"Speak up, man! What in the name of God is going on out there?"

"I—I can't explain it, Dr. Tedrow, but you better—you better get out here right away. It's—it's oh Jee-zus!"

"What *is* it? Stop crying, Wilson, and tell me what the hell is *wrong!*"

"It's, it's number sixteen . . . it's . . ."

"I'll be there in twenty minutes. Keep everyone away from that room. Do you understand? Wilson! Do you understand me?"

"Yessir, yessir. I'll—oh Christ—hurry up Doc . . ."

He could feel his pajama pants bunched around his knees, under his slacks, as he floored the pedal of the ranch wagon. The midnight roads were jerky in the windshield, and the murk that he raced through was almost too grotesque to be a fact of nature.

When he slewed the car into the drive, the gatekeeper threw the iron barrier back almost spastically. The ranch wagon chewed gravel, sending debris back in a wide fan, as Tedrow plunged ahead. When he screeched to a halt before the sanitarium, the doors burst open and the Senior Attendant, Wilson, raced down the steps.

"This way, th-this way, Doctor Te—"

"Get out of my way, you idiot, I know which direction!" he shoved Wilson aside, and strode up the steps and into the building.

"It started about an hour ago . . . we didn't know what was happ—"

"And you didn't call me immediately? Ass!"

"We just thought, we just thought it was another one of his stages, *you* know how he is . . ."

Tedrow snorted in disgust and threw off his topcoat as he made his way rapidly down the corridor to the section of the sanitarium that housed the restraining rooms.

As they came into the annex, through the heavy glass-portaled door, he heard the scream for the first time.

In that scream, in that tormented, pleading, demanding and hopelessly lost tremor there were all the sounds of fear he had ever heard. In that voice he heard even his own voice, his own soul, crying out for something.

For an unnameable something, as the scream came again.

"Give me some light!"

Another world, another voice, another life. Some evil and empty beseeching from a corner of a dust-strewn universe. Hanging there timelessly, vibrant in colorless agony. A million tired and blind stolen voices all wrapped into that one howl, all the eternal sadnesses and losses and pains ever known to man. It was all there, as the good in the world was sliced open and left to bleed its golden fluid away in the dirt. It was a lone animal being eaten by a bird of prey. It was a hundred children crushed beneath iron treads. It was one good man with his entrails in his blood-soaked hands. It was the soul and the pain and the very vital fiber of life, draining away, without light, without hope, without succor.

"Give me some light!"

Tedrow flung himself at the door, and threw back the bolt on the observation window. He stared for a long and silent moment as the scream trembled once more on the air, weightlessly, transparently, tingling off into emptiness. He stared, and felt the impact of a massive horror stifle his own cry of disbelief and terror.

Then he spun away from the window and hung there, sweat-drenched back flat to the wall, with the last sight of Richard Becker he would ever hope to see, burned forever behind his eyes.

The sound of his soft sobs in the corridor held the others back. They stared silently, still hearing that never-spoken echo reverberating down and down and down the corridors of their minds:

Give me some light!

Fumbling beside him, Tedrow slammed the observation window shut, and then his arm sank back to his side.

While inside Room 16, lying up against the far wall, his back against the soft passive padding, Richard Becker looked out at the door, at the corridor, at the world, forever.

Looked out as he had come, purely and simply.

Without a face. From his hairline to his chin, a blank, empty, featureless expanse. Empty. Silent. Devoid of sight or smell or sound. Blank and faceless, a creature God had never deigned to bless with a mirror to the world. His Method now was gone.

Richard Becker, actor, had played his last part, and had gone away, taking with him Richard Becker, a man who had known all the sounds, all the sights, all the life of fear.

*What can I tell you? When I was a kid in Painesville,
Ohio, and involved in the intricacies of Jack Armstrong,
the Green Hornet, I Love A Mystery, Hop Harrigan and
Dick Tracy, anything was possible. Under the side porch
of our house, magic lands of adventure and intrigue made
themselves known to me in the pages of comic books
that chronicled the adventures of the Sandman, Captain
America and Bucky, the Human Torch, the Boy Com-
mandos, Captain Marvel, Starman, Superman, Batman,
Green Lantern, the Flash and (my favorite), Hawkman.
My Saturday afternoons of quivering joy were secretively
spent in the Utopia Theater, that stood next to the
Cleveland Trust, where Kresge's 5 and 10 now looms.
And in that tiny movie house I saw my first Dick Tracy
serial, starring Ralph Byrd. I saw the Shadow with Victor
Jory. I shivered at The Clutching Hand and cheered Don
Winslow Of The Navy and hissed as The Crimson Skull
doomed the hero to a room whose walls came inexorably
together. It was a golden time, before TV, in which the
imagination and the need to be young were coupled with
a world of wonders. In my world, at the corner of Har-
mon Drive and Mentor Avenue, was a wonderful dark
woods, just like the one in*

gnomebody

Did you ever feel your nose running and you wanted
to wipe it, but you couldn't? Most people do, sometime
or other, but I'm different. I let it run.

They call me square. They say, "Smitty, you are a
square. You are so square, you got corners!" This, they
mean, indicates I am an oddball and had better shape up
or ship out. So all right, so I'm a goof-off as far as they
think. Maybe I do get a little sore at things that don't
matter, but if Underfeld hadn't'a layed into me that day
in the gym at school, nothing would have happened. The
trouble is, I get aggravated so easy about little things, like
not making the track team, that I'm no good at studies.
This makes the teachers not care for me even a little.

Besides, I won't take their guff. But that thing with track. It broke me up really good.

There I was standing in the gym, wearing these dirty white gym shorts with a black stripe down the side. And old Underfeld, that's the track coach, he comes up and says, "Whaddaya doin', Smitty?"

Well, anyone with 20-40 eyesight coulda seen what I was doing. I was doing push-ups. "I'm doing push-ups," I said. "Whaddaya think I'm doing? Raising artichokes?"

That was most certainly *not* the time to wise off to old Underfeld. I could see the steam pressure rising in the jerk's manner, and next thing he blows up all over the joint: "Listen, you little punk! Don't get so mouthy with me. In fact, I'm gonna tell you now, 'cause I don't want ya hangin' around the gym or track no more: You just ain't good enough. In a short sprint you got maybe a little guts, but when it comes to a long drag, fifty guys in this school give their right arms to be on the team beat you to the tape. I'm sorry. Get out!"

He is sorry. Like hell!

He is no more sorry than I am as I say, "Ta hell with you, you chowderhead, you got no more brains than these ignorant sprinters that will fall dead before they get to the tape."

Underfeld looks at me like I had stuck him in the seat of his sweat pants with a fistful of pins and kind of gives a gasp, "What did you say?" he inquires, breathless like.

"I don't mumble, do I?" I snapped.

"Get out of here! Get outta here! *Geddouddaere!*"

He was making quite a fuss as I kicked out the door to the dressing rooms.

As I got dressed I gave the whole thing a good think. I was pretty sure that a couple of those stinkin' teachers I had guffed had put wormhead Underfeld up to it. But what can a guy do? I'm just a kid, so says they. They got the cards stacked six ways from Culbertson, and that's it.

I was pretty damned sore as I kicked out the front door. I decided to head for The Woods and try to get it off my mind. That I was cutting school did not bother me. My mother, maybe. But me? No. It was The Woods for me for the rest of the afternoon.

Those Woods. Something funny about them. D'ja ever notice, sometimes right in the middle of a big populated section they got a little stand of woods, real deep and shadowy, you can't see too far into them? You try to figure out why someone hasn't bought up the plot and put a house on it, or why they haven't made it into a playground? Well, that's what my Woods were.

They faced back on a street full of those cracker-box houses constructed by the government, the factory workers shouldn't sleep on the curbs. On the other side, completely boxing them in, was a highway, running straight through to the big town. It isn't really big, but it makes the small town seem not so small.

I used to cut school and go there to read. In the center is a place where everything has that sort of filtery light that seeps down between the tree branches, where there's a big old tree that is strictly one all alone.

What I mean is that tree is great. *Big* thing, stretches and's lost in the branches of the other trees, it's so big. And the roots look like they were forced up out of the ground under pressure, so all's you can see are these sweeping arcs of thick roots, all shiny and risen right out, forming a little bowl under the tree.

Reason I like it so much there, is that it's quieter than anything, and you can feel it. The kind of quiet a library would like to have, but doesn't. To cap all this, the rift in the branches is just big enough so sunlight streams right through and makes a great reading light. And when the sun moves out of that rift, I know it's time to run for home. I make it in just enough time so that Mom doesn't know I was cutting, and thinks I was in school all day.

So last week—I'd been going to The Woods off, on for about two years—I tagged over there, after that creep Underfeld told me I was his last possible choice for the track team. I had a copy of something or other, I don't remember now, I was going to read.

I settled down with my rump stuck into that bowl in the roots, and my feet propped against some smaller rootlings. With that little scrubby plant growth that springs up around the bases of trees, it was pretty comfortable, so I started reading.

Next, you are not going to believe.

I'm sitting there reading, and suddenly I feel this pressure against the seat of my jeans. Next thing I know, I am tumbled over on my head and a trapdoor is opening up out of the ground. Yeah, a trapdoor disguised as solid earth.

Next, you will *really* not believe.

Up out of this hole comes—may I be struck by green lightning if I'm a liar—a gnome! Or maybe he was a elf or a sprite, or some such thing. All I know is that this gnome character is wearing a pair of pegged charcoal slacks, a spread-collar turquoise shirt, green suede loafers, a pork-pie hat with a circumference of maybe three feet, a long, clinky keychain (what the Hell kinda keys could a gnome have?), repulsive loud tie and sun-glasses.

Now maybe you would be too stoned to move, or not believe your eyes, and let a thing like that rock you permanently. But I got a good habit of believing what I see —especially when it's in Technicolor—and besides, more out of reflex than anything else, I grabs.

I'd read some Grimm-type fairy tales, and I know the fable about how if you grab a gnome or a elf, he'll give you what you want, so like I said, I grabs.

I snatch this little character, right around his turquoise collar.

"Hold, man!" says the gnome. "What kinda bit is this? I don't dig this thing *a*tall! Unhand me, Daddy-O!"

"No chance," I answer, kind of in a daze, still not quite sure this is happening to me, "I want a bag of gold or something."

The gnome looks outraged for a second, then he gives a kind of a half laugh and says, "Ho, Diz, you got the wrong cat for this caper. You're comin' on this gig too far and slow! Maybe a fourth-year gnome could hip this gold bit, but me, I'm a party-boy. Flunked outta my Alma Mammy first year. No matriculation—no magiculation! Readin' me, laddy-buck?"

"Uh, yeah, I guess," I ventured, slowly, "you mean you can't give me a bag of gold like in the fairy tale?"

"Fairy tale, schmerry tale. Maybe one ersatz Korean peso, Max, but that is definitely *it*. That is where magic and I parts company. In short, nein, man."

"Hmmm," I hmmmed, tightening my grip a little, he shouldn't get ideas I was letting him get away.

I thought a big think for a minute then I said, "How come you flunked out of school?"

I thought I detected a note of belligerence in the

gnome's voice when he answered, "How would you dig this class stuff, man? Go to class today, go to class tomorrow, yattata-yattata-yat from all these squared-up old codgers what think they are professors? Man, there is so much more else to be doing of note! Real nervous-type stuff like playin' with a jazz combo we got up near campus. You ain't never heard such music!" He appeared to just be starting, "We got a guy on the sackbut what is the coolest. And on dulcimer there is a little troll what can not only send you—but bring you back. And on topa' all this . . ."

I cut him short, "How about this usual free wishes business? Anything to that?"

"I can take a swing at it, man, but like I says, I'm nowhere when it comes to magicking. I'm not the most, if that's the least. Might be a bit sloppy, but I can take a whirl, Earl."

I thought again for a second and then nodded: "Okay," setting him down on the turf, but not yet letting loose his collar, "but no funny business. Just a straight commercial proposition. Three wishes, with no strings, for your freedom."

"Three?" he was incredulous. "Man, *one* is about all this power pack can stand at this late date. No, it would seem that one is my limit, guy. Be taking it or leaving it."

"All right, then, *one*. But no legal loopholes. Let's do it all honest and above-board magic. Deal?"

"Reet!" says he, and races off into The Woods somewhere when I let loose.

I figured he was gone for good, and while I'm waiting, I start to think back on the events of the last few minutes. This is something woulda made Ripley go outta business. The gnome, I figure, is overdue, and so I begin rationalizing why he didn't come back and finally arrive at the conclusion that there is no honor among gnomes. Besides, he had a shifty look to him when he said there would be no tricks in the magic.

But he comes back in a minute, his keychain damn near tripping him up, he's so loaded down with stuff and paraphernalia. Real weird lookin' items, too.

"Copped 'em from the lab over at the U.," he explains, waving a hand at the untidy pile of stuff. "Well, here goes. Remember, there may be more of a mess than is usual with an experienced practitioner, but I'm strictly a goony-bird in this biz, Jack."

"Hey, wait a minute with this magic stuff . . ." I began, but he waved me off impatiently, and began manipulating his implements.

So he starts drawing a star-like thing on the ground, pouring some stinkin' stuff into a cauldron, mixing it up, muttering some gibberish that I could swear had "Oo-bop-shebam" and "Oo-shooby-dooby" in there somewhere, and a lot of other.

Pretty soon he comes over, sprinkles some powder on me, and I sneeze, almost blowing him over.

"Gesundheit," he mutters, staring at me nastily.

He sprinkles some more powder on me, mutters something that sounded like, "By the sacred ring-finger of The Great Gads Bird and Pres, man, hip this kid to what he craveth. Go, go, go, man!"

"Now," he inquires, around a bag in which he is rattling what sounds like bones, "whaddaya want?"

I had been thinking it out, inbetween incantations, and I had decided what I wanted: "Make me so's I can run faster than anyone in the school, willya." I figured then Underfeld would *have* to take me on the team.

The little gnome nods as if he understands, and starts runnin' around and around outside this star-like thing, in ever-decreasing circles, faster n' faster, till I can hardly make him out.

Then he slows down and stops, puffing away like crazy, mumbles something about, "Gotta lay off them clover stems," and so saying throws this pink powder on me, yelling as loud as he can, "FRACTURED!" Up goes a puff of pink smoke and what looks like a side-show magician's magnesium flare, and the next thing I know, he and the stuff is gone, and I'm all alone in The Woods.

So that's the yarn.

Hmmm? What's that? Did he make me so I could run faster than anyone else in the school? Oh, yeah, sure.

You know anybody wants to hire a sixteen-year-old centaur?

When I first arrived in Hollywood in February of 1962 I found myself thinking about the next story frequently. There is no logical reason for its insistent reappearance in my thoughts, except that somehow there seems to me a subtle similarity between the "atmosphere of doom" in the allegory that follows, and the land of the Film Industry. Though everyone out here has been most kind to me, not only in matters of friendship, but in such dandies as giving me large sums of money (most of which I don't deserve), I sometimes wake in the morning expecting to hear a sepulchral voice intoning, "Okay, strike the Hollywood set!" and I'll look out the window to see them rolling up Los Angeles and environs. There is an unreality here that superimposes itself over the normal continuum, effecting a world-view much like that observed through a dessert-dish of Jell-O. Or like the one I cannot seem to forget, in the story I called

the sky is burning

They came flaming down out of a lemon sky, and the first day, ten thousand died. The screams rang in our heads, and the women ran to the hills to escape the sound of it; but there was no escape for them . . . nor for any of us. The sky was aflame with death, and the terrible, unbelievable part of it was . . . the death, the dying was not us!

It started late in the evening. The first one appeared as a cosmic spark struck in the night. Then, almost before the first had faded back into the dusk, there was another, and then another, and soon the sky was a jeweler's pad, twinkling with unnameable diamonds.

I looked up from the Observatory roof, and saw them all, tiny pinpoints of brilliance, cascading down like raindrops of fire. And somehow, before any of it was explained, I knew: this was something important. Not important the way five extra inches of plastichrome on the tail-fins of a new copter are important . . . not important the way a war is important . . . but important the way the creation of the Universe had been important, the way the death of it would be. And I knew it was happening all over Earth.

There could be no doubt of that. All across the horizon, as far as I could see, they were falling and burning and burning. The sky was not appreciably brighter, but it was as though a million new stars had been hurled up there to live for a brief microsecond.

Even as I watched, Portales called to me from below. "Frank! Frank, come down here . . . this is fantastic!"

I swung down the catwalk into the telescope dome, and saw him hunched over the refraction eyepiece. He was pounding his fist against the side of the vernier adjustment box. It was a pounding of futility, and strangeness. A pounding without meaning behind it. "Look at this, Frank. Will you take a look at this?" His voice was a rising inflection of disbelief.

I nudged him aside and slid into the bucket. The scope was trained on Mars. The Martian sky was burning, too. The same pinpoints of light, the same intense pyrotechnics spiraling down. We had alloted the evening to a study of the red planet, for it was clear in that direction, and I saw it all very sharply, as brightnesses and darkness again, all across the face of the planet.

"Call Bikel at Wilson," I told Portales. "Ask him about Venus."

Behind me I heard Portales dialing the closed circuit number, and I half-listened to his conversation with Aaron Bikel at Mt. Wilson. I could see the flickering reflections of the vid-screen on the phone, as they washed across the burnished side of the scope. But I didn't turn around; I knew what the answer would be.

Finally, he hung up, and the colors died: "The same," he said sharply, as though defying me to come up with an answer. I didn't bother snapping back at him. He had been bucking for my job as Director of the Observatory for nearly three years now, and I was accustomed to his antagonisms—desperately as I had to machinate occasionally, to keep him in his place.

I watched for a while longer, then left the dome.

I went downstairs, and tuned in my short-wave radio, trying to find out what Tokyo or Heidelburg or Johannesburg had to say. I wasn't able to catch any mention of the phenomena during the short time I fiddled with the sweep, but I was certain they were seeing it the same everywhere else.

Then I went back to the Dome, to change the settings on the scope.

After an argument with Portales, I beamed the scope down till it was sharp to just inside the atmospheric blanket. I tipped in the sweeper, and tried a fast scan of the sky, but continued to miss the bursts of light at the moment of their explosion. So I cut in the photo mechanism, and set a wide angle to it. Then I cut off the sweep, and started clicking them off. I reasoned that the frequency of the lights would inevitably bring one into photo focus.

Then I went downstairs, and back to the short-wave. I spent two hours with it, and managed to pick up a news broadcast from Switzerland. I had been right, of course.

Portales rang me after two hours and said we had a full reel of photos, and should he have them developed. This was too big to trust to his adolescent whims, and rather than have him fog up a valuable photo, I told him to leave them in the container, and I'd be right up, to handle it myself.

When the photos came out of the solution, I had to finger through thirty or forty of empty space before I caught ten that had what I wanted.

They were not meteorites.

On the contrary.

Each of the flames in the sky was a creature. A living creature. But not human. Far from it.

The photos told what they looked like, but not till the Project Snatch ship went up and sucked one off the sky did we realize how large they were, that they glowed with an inner light of their own and—that they were telepathic.

From what I can gather, it was no problem capturing one. The ship opened its cargo hatch, and turned on the sucking mechanisms used to drag in flotsam from space. The creature, however, could have stopped itself from being dragged into the ship, merely by placing one of its seven-taloned hands on either side of the hatch, and resisting the sucker. But it was interested, as we learned later; it had been five thousand years, and they had not known we had come so far, and the creature was interested. So it came along.

When they called me in, along with five hundred-odd other scientists (and Portales managed to wangle himself a place in the complement, through that old charlatan Senator Gouverman), we went to the Smithsonian, where they had had him installed, and marveled . . . just stood and marveled.

He—or she, we never knew—resembled the Egyptian god Ra. It had the head of a hawk, or what appeared to be a hawk, with great slitted eyes of green in which flecks of crimson and amber and black danced. Its body was thin to the point of emaciation, but humanoid with two arms and two legs. There were bends and joints on the body where no such bends and joints existed on a human, but there was a definite chest cavity, and obvious buttocks, knees, and chin. The creature was a pale, milky-white, except on the hawk's-crest which was a brilliant blue, fading down into white. Its beak was light blue, also blending into the paleness of its flesh. It had seven toes to the foot, seven talons to the hand.

The God Ra. God of the Sun. God of light.

The creature glowed from within with a pale, but distinct aura that surrounded it like a halo. We stood there, looking up at it in the glass cage. There was nothing to say; there it was, the first creature from another world. We might be going out into space in a few years—farther, that is, than the Moon, which we had reached in 1963, or Mars that we had circumnavigated in 1966—but for now, as far as we knew, the Universe was wide and without end, and out there we would find unbelievable creatures to rival any imagining. But this was the first.

We stared up at it. The being was thirteen feet tall.

Portales was whispering something to Karl Leus from Caltech. I snorted to myself at the way he never gave up; for sheer guff and grab I had to hand it to him. He was a pusher all right. Leus wasn't impressed. It was apparent he wasn't interested in what Portales had to say, but he had been a Nobel Prize winner in '63 and he felt obligated to be polite to even obnoxious pushers like my assistant.

The army man—whatever his name was—was standing

on a platform near the high, huge glass case in which the creature stood, unmoving, but watching us.

They had put food of all sorts through a feeder slot, but it was apparent the creature would not touch it. It merely stared down, silent as though amused, and unmoving as though uncaring.

"Gentlemen, gentlemen, may I have your attention!" the Army man caroled at us. A slow silence, indicative of our disrespect for him and his security measures that had caused us such grief getting into this meeting, fell through the groups of men and women at the foot of the case.

"We have called you here—" pompous ass with his *we*, as if he were the government incarnate, "to try and solve the mystery of who this being is, and what he has come to Earth to find out. We detect in this creature a great menace to—" and he went on and on, bleating and parodying all the previous scare warnings we had had about every nation on Earth. He could not have realized how we scoffed at him, and wanted to hoot him off the platform. This creature was no menace. Had we not captured him, her, it—the being would have burnt to a cinder like its fellows, falling into our atmosphere.

So we listened him to the end. Then we moved in closer and stared at the creature. It opened its beak in what was uncommonly like a smile, and I felt a shiver run through me. The sort of shiver I get when I hear deeply emotional music, or the sort of shiver I get when making love. It was a basic trembling in the fibers of my body. I can't explain it, but it was a prelude to something. I paused in my thinking, just ceased my existence if *Cogito Ergo Sum* is the true test of existence. I stopped thinking and allowed myself to sniff of that strangeness; to savor the odor of space and faraway worlds, and one world in particular.

A world where the winds are so strong, the inhabitants have hooks on their feet, which they dig into the firm green soil to maintain their footing. A world where colors riot among the foliage one season, and the next—are the pale white of a maggot's flesh. A world where the triple moons swim through azure skies, and sing in their passage, playing on a lute of invisible strings, the seas and the deserts as accompanists. A world of wonder, older than Man and older than the memory of the Forever.

I realized abruptly, as my mind began to function once more, that I had been listening to the creature. Ithk was the creature's—name?—denomination?—gender?—something. It was one of five hundred hundred-thousand like itself, who had come to the system of Sol.

Come? No, perhaps that was the wrong word. They had *been* . . .

Not by rockets, nothing that crude. Nor space-warp, nor even mental power. But a leap from their world—what was that name? Something the human tongue could not form, the human mind could not conceive?—to this world in seconds. Not instantaneous, for that would have involved machinery of some sort, or the expenditure of mental power. It was beyond that, and above that. It was an *essence* of travel. But they had come. They had come across the mega-galaxies, hundreds of thousands of light-years . . . incalculable distances from there to here, and Ithk was one of them.

Then it began to talk to some of us.

Not all of us there, for I could tell some were not receiving it. I don't attribute it to good or bad in any of us, nor intelligence, nor even sensitivity. Perhaps it was whim on Ithk's part, or the way he(?) wanted to do it out of necessity. But whatever it was, he spoke to only some of us there. I could see Portales was receiving nothing, though old Karl Leus's face was in a state of rapture, and I knew he had the message himself.

For the creature was speaking in our minds telepathically. It did not amaze me, or confound me, nor even shock me. It seemed right. It seemed to go with Ithk's size and look, its aura and arrival.

And it spoke to us.

And when it was done, some of us crawled up on the platform and released the bolts that held the case of glass shut; though we all knew Ithk could have left it at any second had it desired. But Ithk had been interested in knowing—before it burned itself out as its fellows had done—and it had found out about us little Earth people. It had satisfied its curiosity, on this instant's stopover before it went to hurtling, flaming destruction. It had been curious . . . for the last time Ithk's people had come here,

Earth had been without creatures who went into space. Even as pitifully short a distance into space as we could venture.

But now the stopover was finished, and Ithk had a short journey to complete. It had come an unimaginably long way, for a purpose, and though this had been interesting, Ithk was anxious to join his fellows.

So we unbolted the cage—which had never *really* confined a creature that could *be* out of it at will—and Ithk was there! not there. Gone!

The sky was still flaming.

One more pinpoint came into being suddenly, slipped down in a violent rush through the atmosphere, and burned itself out like a wasting torch. Ithk was gone.

Then we left.

Karl Leus leaped from the thirty-second story of a building in Washington that evening. Nine others died that day. And though I was not ready for that, there was a deadness in me. A feeling of waste and futility and hopelessness. I went back to the Observatory, and tried to drive the memory of what Ithk had said from my mind and my soul. If I had been as deeply perceptive as Leus or any of the other nine, I might have gone immediately. But I am not in their category. They realized the full depth of what it had said, and so perceiving, they had taken their lives. I can understand their doing it.

Portales came to me when he heard about it.

"They just—just *killed* themselves!" he babbled. I was sick of his petty annoyances. Sick of them, and not even interested any longer in fighting him.

"Yes, they killed themselves," I answered wearily, staring at the flaming, burning sky from the Observatory catwalk. It always seemed to be night now. Always night—with light.

"But *why?* Why would they do it?"

I spoke to hear my thoughts. For I knew what was coming. "Because of what the creature said."

"What it said?"

"What it told us, and what it did not tell us."

"It *spoke* to you?"

"To some of us. To Leus and the nine and others. I heard it."

"But why didn't *I* hear it? I was right there!"

I shrugged. He had not heard, that was all.

"Well, what did it say? Tell me," he demanded.

I turned to him, and looked at him. Would it affect him? No, I rather thought not. And that was good. Good for him, and good for others like him. For without them, Man would cease to exist. I told him.

"The lemmings," I said. "You know the lemmings. For no reason, for some deep instinctual surging, they follow each other, and periodically throw themselves off the cliffs. They follow one another down to destruction. A racial trait. It was that way with the creature and his people. They came across the mega-galaxies to kill themselves here. To commit mass suicide in our solar system. To burn up in the atmosphere of Mars and Mercury and Venus and Earth, and to die, that's all. Just to die."

His face was stunned. I could see he comprehended that. But what did it matter? That was not what had made Leus and the nine kill themselves, that was not what filled me with such a feeling of frustration. The drive of one race was not the drive of another.

"But—but—I don't underst—"

I cut him off.

"That was what Ithk said."

"But why did they come *here* to die?" he asked, confused. "Why *here* and not some other solar system or galaxy?"

That was what Ithk had said. That was what we had wondered in our minds—damn us for asking—and in its simple way, Ithk had answered.

"Because," I explained slowly, softly, "this is the end of the Universe."

His face did not register comprehension. I could see it was a concept he could not grasp. That the solar system, Earth's system, the backyard of Earth to be precise, was the end of the Universe. Like the flat world over which Columbus would have sailed, into nothingness. This was the end of it all. Out there, in the other direction, lay a known Universe, with an end to it . . . but they— Ithk's people—ruled it. It was theirs, and would always be theirs. For they had racial memory burnt into each embryo child born to their race, so they would never stagnate. After every lemming race, a new generation was born, that would live for thousands of years, and advance. They would go on till they came here to flame out in our atmosphere. But they would rule what they had while they had it.

So to us, to the driving, unquenchably curious, seeking and roaming Earthman, whose life was tied up with wanting to know, *needing* to know, there was nothing left. Ashes. The dust of our own system. And after that, nothing.

We were at a dead end. There could be no wandering among the stars. It was not that we *couldn't* go. We could. But we would be tolerated. It was *their* Universe, and this, our Earth, was the dead end.

Ithk had not known what it was doing when it said that to us. It had meant no evil, but it had doomed some of us. Those of us who dreamed. Those of us who wanted more than what Portales wanted.

I turned away from him and looked up.

The sky was burning.

I held very tightly to the bottle of sleeping tablets in my pocket. So much light up there.

©Lorillard 1974

KENT

King Size or
Deluxe 100's.

Micronite filter.
Mild, smooth taste.
America's quality cigarette.
Kent.

Try the crisp, clean taste of Kent Menthol.

The only Menthol with the famous Micronite filter.

Kings: 16 mg. "tar," 1.0 mg. nicotine;
100's: 18 mg. "tar," 1.2 mg. nicotine;
Menthol: 18 mg. "tar," 1.2 mg. nicotine;
av. per cigarette, FTC Report Mar. '74.

Warning: The Surgeon General Has Determined That Cigarette Smoking Is Dangerous to Your Health.

Bluntly put, the following story has truly been used. I am always astounded at writers who sell and re-sell and re-re-sell their stories or books, wringing every last possible penny from them. But in the case of the following epic, I can truly say I take backseat to no man. The idea occurred to me in my first days at Ohio State University, back in the early Fifties. I wrote it and it was published in the Ohio State Sundial, *the humor magazine I later edited. When I got to New York in 1956, I submitted the idea as story-continuity to EC Publications, now the producers of* Mad *magazine, then the producers of such goodies as* Weird Science-Fantasy *comics, in which this story appeared as "Upheaval." Between these two appearances, however, the story showed up in the amateur science fiction magazine I published,* Dimensions. *In that incarnation it was called "Green Odyssey." Eventually, I wrote it as a full short story and it appeared in Bill Hamling's short-lived* Space Travel Magazine. *No two of these setting-downs were alike, incidentally. Then the radio performance rights were purchased by an outfit that was planning to revive* Dimension X *for Sunday listening on the Mutual Broadcasting System. It never got off the ground, but I had been paid, so that was another sale. There may have been another conversion or two of this story, but I can't remember right now if such was the case. What I do remember is that the basic tenet of this story—You ain't as hot an item as you think, Chollie!—has appealed to every editor who has seen it. Which speaks well for mankind, I guess, if you think there's validity in the encounter viewed in*

mealtime

While the ship *Circe* burned its way like some eternal Roman Candle through the surrounding dark of forever, within:

"You make me sick, Dembois! Absolutely sick to my gut!"

"Sick? Why you sleazy crumb, I ought to break you in half! Who the hell do you think you're—"

"All right! Now! That's it from the both of you. I've got enough on my hands now with just getting there and back—I said knock it *off*, Kradter—just getting there and back, and I've heard enough swill from both of you on this trip! So kill it before I take a spanner to your heads. Read me?"

There were three of them riding the flame to the stars. Three on a Catalog Ship sent to chart the planets of unknown stars, and to take brief studies of the worlds themselves. They were three months out, on a jump between their last world—an ivy-covered ball of green they had named Garbo because it was the single planet of its star—and their next one, which had no name. Nor chart position; nor star whose light had reached the Earth as yet. But there was another island of star clusters across this immensity of black between galaxies, and as soon as they had hopped it through Inverspace, they would find yet another shining light to draw them on.

It had been that way for over one year and nine months. They had catalogued over two-hundred and twenty worlds, each one different from its predecessors.

But the work was not enough. Time hangs like an albatross about the neck of the space-wanderer. He sees blackness all about him, and occasionally the starshine, and even more occasionally the crazy-quilt patchwork that is Inverspace. There is no radio contact with Earth. There is little recreation and even less provision made to keep fit and alert.

But nature knows when its creatures need sharpening. So, the arguments.

There were three of them: Kradter, who was descended from Prussians, and had the look of them. Tall, with heavily-muscled torso and the square, close-cropped blonde hair of his ancestors. Rigid in his thinking unless pried forcibly from the clutch of his convictions. Poverty and determination had combined to bring him into the high-paying but dangerous SeekServ branch of the Navy. He was a Lieutenant, with the opinion that rank was unimportant, only drive was essential.

The second was Dembois, who was a bigot.

He came from Louisiana wealth, and his background was one of idleness, dissipation and revelry. A serious affair with a lovely quadroon girl had forced his father to order the boy out of the city, and into the Navy. Authority and wealth and position had saved Dembois from a prison sentence, but for him the Navy was sentence enough. He despised the SeekServ, and it was for that reason he had joined it. Self-punishment, in the adolescent "Look how I'm suffering, aren't you sorry you threw me out of the house!" tradition had prompted his signing-on. He loathed the furry and tracked and tentacled and finned and feathered aliens he discovered on the worlds of space.

He hated Negros and Jews, Catholics and Orientals. He was uncomfortable in the presence of poor people, sick people, crippled people or hungry people. Yet there was a fierce determination in him, also. What he wanted to do, he did thoroughly and well; what he did not want to do, but knew he *must* do, he did in a similar fashion. He was an Ensign II.

The third was the Captain of the *Circe*.

His past was the reflective, mysterious face of a mirror; any man might look, but all he would see was the image of himself. No more. His past was silent in its shell, but its form was there to be seen in the man. His name was Calk.

His personality dominated the *Circe*, held the other two in check. Calk was strong, perhaps too strong for his own good. The bickering was beginning to tell on him.

"What the hell was it all about *this* time?"

Dembois and Kradter spoke together, their voices rising automatically in anger as they found competition. Calk was forced to shut them up again. Then he motioned to Kradter. "Okay. You first. What was it this time?"

Kradter looked disgruntled, and yanked his pipe from where it was thrust pistol-like in his belt. He dug a finger into the blackened bowl and growled something unintelligible.

"Well, now look, Kradter, if you want to say something, say it. If you don't, there isn't an argument, nothing to settle, and I can go the blazes back to my plot-tank."

Kradter looked up, as though ready to throw a string of cursewords, but merely said, instead, "We were arguing the nobility of Man."

Calk's eyebrows went up. They were thick and black,

and struck the impression of two slanted caterpillars inching up his forehead.

Kradter explained hurriedly, expecting Dembois to burst in momentarily. "I was saying that the poor slobs we find on these worlds *deserve* human care. It's our *obligation* to these lesser creatures to provide them with the comforts a greater race can offer."

Dembois snorted, and Calk looked over sharply. "Now, what was your beef, that you wanted to start a brawl?"

Dembois looked angrily at Kradter. "And I say it's not our place to do *any*thing for these stinking savages. The only thing we owe them is conquest. They'd overrun us in a month if we gave them the chance. Kill the bloody bastards, that's the answer to colonial expansion out here.

"Put them away for good, the first thing we see them. It's the only way we can be sure we're protected. This ass—" he stopped at Kradter's bleat of anger, and tensed as the other man took a half-step forward.

Calk stopped them. "Okay, knock it off. So one of you thinks we should play Big Daddy to the poor natives, and the other thinks we should mow 'em down on sight. Okay. Fine. Good. Now shut your traps and let me get our plot set, or we'll wind up frying inside some sun when we popout."

He gave them both a strange look, and murmured, *"Homo superior,"* and walked out of the lounge.

The other two sat staring at points between them. Neither spoke. No crossbow bolts were loosed.

The *Circe* moved out.

A green fog in the ever-changing pattern of Inverspace. Green, roiling, oily dark fog.

A speck of crimson that flickered and steadied and exploded into sharp golden fragments.

A lurch, a twist, the guts heaving and the puke-masks filling, and the eyeballs burning without heat. The roots of the hair straining, and the arches of the cheekbones stretching the skin tight as a corpse's. Then a grey-out, a black-out, a white-and-black-out and the ship was traveling in the normal universe again.

They were in sight of the cold, chiselled stars and the steady multi-colored stars. They were a Catalog Ship and there was work to be done. The constellation firmed out in the plot-tank, superimposing itself almost exactly over Calk's lined-in course. The CourseComp chattered eerily and the few discrepancies in course variation were merged, so that the wing-shaped constellation was directly on the Captain's pattern.

Dembois and Kradter knocked politely on the door to the control cabin, and slid it open when Calk said absently, "Come."

"How's it set?" Dembois asked.

"About three points off, but we've corrected already," Calk replied, indicating the plot-tank. He slipped the infrared goggles off and stuck them on their pad. "You start undogging the gear yet?"

Kradter nodded, addressing the nod totally to Calk, and Dembois's lips pursed in annoyance that the conversation had been stolen away from him. He thrust back into it with, "I hope we don't run up against any eetees. The last batch was enough to turn my stomach for quite a while."

Kradter whirled on him again. "I thought we had this out once and for all, man. I thought you understood our job is to befriend and aid these unfortunate—"

"Bull!" Dembois snarled. "Show me in the Regs where it says that? Show me, or shut your Heinie trap—eetee lover."

Kradter had swung before Calk could stop him. He caught Dembois along the cheekbone and spun the smaller man. The Ensign II staggered backward, crashed into the bulkhead and slid to one knee, shaking his head. Kradter was moving forward when Calk caught him, slipping his hands under the Prussian's armpits and up behind his neck, where they locked. He dragged Kradter half off the floor in a full-nelson and shook him solidly, taking the Lieutenant's breath away.

"Now . . . knock . . . off . . . that . . . stuff!" Calk whispered loudly in Kradter's ear. He held the man completely paralyzed, his feet dangling a quarter inch off the floor. Tremendous muscles stood out on Calk's arms, beneath the sleeves of his T-shirt, and a blue pulse of nerve throbbed at his right temple.

Dembois staggered erect, clutching his face, and made a few idle stepping motions; then, in a blur, he hurled himself at Kradter and sank a doubled fist into the Lieutenant's belly. Kradter gasped and moaned softly and slumped in Calk's grasp.

The Captain dropped him, reached over with one hand and brought a judo cut down on the Ensign's neck. Dembois clattered to the deckplates beside his adversary.

Calk returned to the plotting seat, and snapped his goggles back on. Once more he murmured softly to himself: *"Homo superior!"*

The three outer planets were catalogued without difficulty. The blue dwarf was not able to reach them with its rays, and they were frozen; but there were deep treasures of pitchblende and phosphorous and trace elements from which ferro-zinc could be collandered and strained with little effort. They were marked in the log as triple-A planets, well worth the trouble to reach and mine.

The center ring of planets—fifteen of them—was not as worthwhile. There were three desert worlds (too much harsh silicon), seven barren rock worlds without atmosphere, and ignored by the hand of God (nothing grew there, nothing of value), four jungle planets (one with technicolored tyrannosauri), and one oddity.

They saved the oddity for last.

Before they would catalogue the inner round of worlds —there appeared to be nineteen, though one of those they credited as being a moon of a blue and white planet might have had an atmosphere of its own—they would set down and explore the oddity.

The oddity was a pale silver globe without ground feature and without atmosphere. It was a great ball of smooth tinfoil set in the black of space, a featureless plain without hump or depression, mountain or valley, stream or even rock formation. No grass and no clouds. In fact, nothing.

They stared down at the planet inching its way to greatness in the ports. It was as though they were settling toward a gigantic beachball.

"That's impossible!" Dembois gasped.

"How can it be impossible, you clown? It's there, isn't it?" Kradter was spoiling for another fight. The pains in his stomach had not yet completely left him.

"Break!" Calk snapped. "Not this close to landfall, you two. And it may be impossible, but it's there, and we have to check it out. No telling *what* a planet like that might have beneath the surface."

Dembois cast a sharp glance at the potentiometer and the gauging devices for composition. "They say you're wrong, Captain."

Calk turned to the dials and studied them at length. They read zero. Not negative, as they read in space, but zero. But that, too, was impossible. The planet had to be made of *something*.

They looked at each other, and said nothing, for there was nothing to say. They had encountered a phenomenon. "Could it be contra-terrene?" The question hung unasked in the air of the control room. The only way to answer it was to test.

They shot out the missile when they were still ten miles above the smooth silver surface, and it sped down down down without hindrance of air or course correction. It hit, and exploded. But its indestructible plasteel devices continued to register on the *Circe*'s banks, so it was apparent the planet was of matter, not the anti-matter that would disintegrate the rocket on contact.

They landed.

When the three men emerged from the ship, sliding down the landing ramp as children on a playground slide, they were encased in bulky pressure suits and clear bubble helmets. Each carried a triple-thread stun-rifle, for despite the utterly safe appearance of the planet, there was no question as to carrying weapons. Space was deep and angry at Man. Its creatures were varied and utterly unpredictable. So they never took a chance.

As they walked out across the featureless plain, their chest-consoles humming and gauging and studying, they moved in a tight triangle.

Calk, in the front, as the apex of the triangle, cast about warily, his triple-threader swinging in lazy arcs.

"Have you noticed the ground?" Kradter asked, his voice hushed and solemn as a man in a cathedral, transmitted over the intercom system.

Calk nodded, but Dembois put it into words.

"It's spongey. Springy. Like the 'giving' floors back at SeekServ Central. What's it made of?"

"I don't know," Calk answered, and that was the final word any of them said.

There was a shivering in the planet. A soft trembling, like a bowl of jelly. It shivered and pulsed and seemed to deepen as they stopped.

Then, through their intercoms, they heard a distinct crunch and clang, and as one they spun around. Half a mile behind them the *Circe* was trembling, tottering, falling, and then—

The planet swallowed the ship.

They screamed. Each of them, and the pitch was the same. The meaning behind the screams was the same. They were lost, stranded out here, somewhere out in the nowhere, with only the oxygen in their tanks to sustain them, and their transportation gone!

Then . . . they realized the greater danger. *The planet was carnivorous!*

They realized it too late.

Beneath their feet, the ground swelled, like a bubble bursting, and abruptly opened with a wet, smacking sound . . .

Their screams were cut short as they fell fell fell— and the silver, featureless, spongey ground closed without a break. Without an indication that a ship of space and three men had been there.

In the syrup. Grey and all-consuming. Heaving, tumbling, dragged deeper and deeper, thrust into the maw of a force without form. The allness was about them; they were being . . .

EATEN ALIVE!!

The grey substance held them in a rubbery grip. They could move but slightly. Grey and sparkling, coating their helmets. Breathing was clear, but seemed so oppressive. The planet of grey featurelessness was alive, the entire world was a creature, an entity, and they were in its gut. They turned over and over wishing knowing hoping not caring but knowing that this was all of it down to the bottom without end and without hope and hands out and legs out and their fingers spread and their eyes wide as their throats tensed and tore at the screams that rattled within their helmets . . .

Overhead, the *Circe* swam into view, was there a moment, no longer, and gone out out and out gone again in the silver nothingness that lived held would not release them goodbye.

The trembling was coming again. Suddenly. Then they felt the planet around them heaving, tremors starting low and roiling, spilling, sucking upward. They had no hope. In a few minutes the air must surely give out, for they had been down in the heart of this living world for eons, centuries, eternities, and when the air went, they would die. The pricklings at their skin told them the digestive fluids of the planet were even now trying to assimilate the fabric of the bulky pressure suits. But there was the heaving . . .

And they felt themselves rising, speeding as they rose, and the silver was growing lighter and lighter and with no warning they were

POP!

thrown up and out of the planet, like corks shooting to the surface of a lake, and they fell back to the sponged surface. They were free.

The planet trembled violently, agitated beyond belief. Like pebbles they were flipped and tossed and hurled and thrown, bouncing bouncing bouncing. The *Circe* emerged from the planet, two hundred feet away, lying on its side, being jostled and caromed as they were.

Without hesitation they scrambled madly for the ship, and threw themselves through the lock. Fighting the unending bouncing and jostling movement of the mad planet they got to the controls and the dampers went in and the fire chambers spurted—

The *Circe* blasted off without care of course, the men thanking God for their lives, thanking Providence for the inexplicable release from sure death.

Behind them, the silver planet settled slowly, and the trembling ceased. It was silent and solid once more.

Kradter was still sheet-white.

"We've got to get back into contact with Earth!"

Dembois's voice quavered. "That *thing* is a horror! A menace! We've got to get Earth to burn it out of space!"

Calk's laughter stopped them. They stared at him, for the first real signs of emotion were contorting the Captain's face. His roars of mirth broke against the bulkheads and tinkled like dust motes about them. For a second they thought of hysteria and slapping him, but when Kradter took a step forward, Calk waved him away with a mirth-weakened hand.

Finally, he stopped, sucking in breath, and clutching his sides. "Oh, you two give me *such* a pain in the ass!" he laughed. Then his face went rigid again. His voice steadied and he looked at them. "Don't you know even yet? Don't you understand what's happened?" They stared at him, uncomprehending.

"All the way out here," he said, bitterness living in his words, "you've been telling me how great and wonderful man is. How he rules the universe, how it's his job to show eetees the way, or destroy them. As though Man were the end-product of the life race, as though we were at the pinnacle of development. You never could have considered that there was a higher life-form than us."

"What are you talking about," Dembois snapped. "Are you crazy?"

Calk's face was angry, really angry, as he said: "You asses! You conceited, self-important asses. Don't you understand what I'm saying? *Homo superior,* ha! That's the joke of the century. You fools, can't you see . . .

"Man has just had the greatest insult of all thrown at him!

"That planet *vomited* us up!"

You know the world is going to end. There's no question about it, no supposition, no ravings from a bushy-bearded fanatic that may prove false . . . this is the real thing, we all go splat a week from next Wednesday. What do you do? What if you were a young man who had never enjoyed the manifest pleasures of a woman's body? What if you had been hidebound and stultified all your days, when you got wind of the coming Boom? What then? Why, perhaps you would follow a course of action similar to the hero of this little piece, in which I tried to say that everything is relative, and even dross, under the proper conditions, can be as good as gold. And you know, it's indicative of our current Clipster Culture that very often the ones who would rob are the ones who get robbed, the fleecers get fleeced, and hyprocrisy counts for nothing when the chips are down. In other words, the love of a less than kindly creature can be the single most important possession in the universe, on

the very last day of a
good woman

Finally, he knew the world was going to end. It had grown in certainty with terrible slowness. His was not a perfect talent; but rather, a gem with many small flaws in it. Had he been able to see the future clearly, had he not been a partial clairvoyant, his life might not have come to what it had.

His hunger would not have been what it was.

Yet the brief, fogged glimpses were molded together, and he knew the Earth was about to end. By the same rude certainty that told him it was going to end, he knew it was not self-deception—it was not merely *his* death. It was the final, irrevocable finis of his world, with every life upon it. This he saw in a shattered fragment of clarity, and he knew it would come in two weeks, on a Thursday night.

His name was Arthur Fulbright, and he wanted a woman.

How strange or odd. To know the future. To know it in that most peculiar of fashions: not as a unified whole, as a superimposed something on the image of now, but in bits and snatches, in fits and starts. In humming, deliberate quicknesses (*a truck will come around the corner in a moment*) making him (*Carry Back will win*) almost a denizen of two worlds (*the train will leave ten minutes early*) he saw the future through a glass darkly (*you will find your other cuff link in the medicine cabinet*) and was hardly aware of what this power promised.

For years, a soft, brown shambling man all hummed words and gentle glances, living with his widowed mother in an eight room house set about with honeysuckle and sweet pea. For years, to work in a job of unidentifiable type and station; for years, returning to the house and the comforting pastel of Mother.

Years that held little change, little activity, little of note or importance. Yet good years, smooth years, and silent.

Then Mother had died. Sighing in the night, she had slowed down like a phonograph, like the old crank phonograph covered under a white sheet in the attic, and had died. Life had played its melody for her, and just as naturally, ended.

For Arthur it had meant changes, and most of all, it had meant emptiness.

Now no more the nights of sound sleep, the evenings of quiet discussion and backgammon or whist, the afternoons of lunch prepared in time for a return to the office, the mornings with cinnamon toast and orange juice ready. Now it was a single lane highway, that he had to travel alone.

Learning to eat in restaurants, learning where the clean linens were kept, sending his clothes out to be mended and cleaned.

And most of all, coming to realize in the six years since Mother's death, that he could see the future once in a while. It was in no way alarming, nor even—after living with it so long—surprising. The word terrifying, in connection with his sight of the future, would never have occurred to him, had he not seen that night of flame and death, the end of the world.

But he did see it, and it made a difference.

Because now that he was about to die, now that he had two weeks and no more, he had to find a purpose. There had to be a reason to die without regret. Yet here he sat, in the high-backed wing chair in the darkened living room, with the empty eight room house around him, and there was no purpose. He had not considered his own demise; Mother's going had been hard enough to reconcile, but he had known it would come some day (though the ramifications of her death had never dawned on him). His own death was something else.

"How can a man come to thirty-four years old, and have nothing?" he asked himself. "How can it be?"

It was true, of course. He had nothing. No talent, no mark to leave on affairs, no wake, no purpose.

And with the tallying of his lacks, he came to the most important one of all. The one marking him as not yet a man, no matter what he thought. The lack of a woman. He was a virgin, he had never had a woman.

With two weeks left on Earth, Arthur Fulbright knew what he wanted, more than anything, more than fame or wealth or position. His desire for his last days on Earth was a simple one, an uncluttered one.

Arthur Fulbright wanted a woman.

There had been a little money. Mother had left over two thousand dollars in cash and savings bonds. He had been able to put away another two thousand in his own account. That made four thousand dollars, and it became very important, but not till later.

The idea of buying a woman came to him after many other considerations. The first attempt was with a young woman of his acquaintance, who worked as a steno-typist in the office, in the billing section.

"Jackie," he asked her, having passed time on occasion, "would you—uh—how would you like to go to a—uh—show with me tonight . . . or something?"

She stared at him curiously, seeing a cipher; and having mentally relegated the evening to Scrabble with a girl friend, accepted.

That evening she doubled her fist and gave him such a blow beneath his rib cage, that his eyes watered and his side hurt for almost an hour.

The next day he avoided the girl with the blonde,

twirled pony-tail who was browsing in the HISTORICAL
NOVELS section of the Public Library. He had had a
glimpse often enough—of the future—to know what this
one meant. She was married, despondent, and did not
wear her ring through hostility of her husband. He saw
himself in an unpleasant situation, involving the girl, the
librarian, and the library guard. He avoided the library.

As the week wore through, as Arthur realized he had
never developed the techniques other men used to snare
girls, he knew his time was running out. As he walked the
streets, late at night, passing few people, but still people
who were soon to perish in a flaming death, he knew his
time was slipping away with terrible swiftness.

Now it was no mere desire. Now it was a drive, an
urge within him that consumed his thoughts, that moti-
vated him as nothing else in life ever had. And he cursed
Mother for her fine, old Southern ways, for her white
flesh that had bound him in umbilical attention. Her never-
demanding, always-pleasant ways, that had made it so
simple to live on in that pastel world of strifeless, effort-
less complacency.

To die a-flaming with the rest of the world . . . empty.

The streets were chill, and the lampposts had wavering,
unearthly halos about them. From far off came the sound
of a car horn, lost in the darkness; and a truck, its diesel
gut rumbling, shifted into gear as a stop light changed,
and coughed away. The pavement had the sick pallor of
rotting flesh, and the stars were lost in inkiness on a
moonless night. He bunched himself tightly inside his topcoat, and bent into the vague, leaf-picking breeze slanting
toward him. A dog somewhere howled briefly, and a door
slammed on another block. Abruptly, he was ultra-sensi-
tive to these sounds, and wanted to be part with them, inside with the love and humor of a home. But had he been
a pariah, a criminal, a leper, he could not have been more
alone. He tickled the philosophy of his culture, that allowed men such as himself to mature without direction,
without hope, without love. Which he needed so desperately.

At the intersection, halfway down the block, a girl
emerged from shadows, her high heels tock tock tocking
rhythmically on the sidewalk, then the street, as she
stepped across, and went her way.

He was cutting across the lawn of a house, and converging on her from right angles before he realized what he was doing, what his intentions were. By then, his momentum had carried him.

Rape.

The word flowered in his mind like a hot-house flower, with blood-red petals, grew to monstrous proportions, and withered, black at the edges, even as he scooted briskly, head down and hands in coat pockets, toward her direction of progress.

Could he do it? Could he carry it off? She was young and beautiful, desirable, he knew. She would have to be. He would take her down on the grass, and she would not scream, but would be pliant and acquiescent. She had to be.

He raced ahead of where she would meet him, and he lay down on the moist, brown earth, within the cover of bushes, to wait for her. In the distance he could hear her heels counting off the steps till he was upon her.

Then, even as his desire ate at him, other pictures came. A twisted, half-naked body lying in the street, a mob of men screaming and brandishing a rope, a picture of Mother, her face ashen and transfigured with horror. He crammed his eyes shut, and pressed his cheek to the ground. It was the all-mother, consoling him. He was the child who had done wrong, and his need was great. The all-mother comforted him, directed him, caressed him with propriety and deep devotion. He lay there as the girl clacked past.

The heat in his face died away, and it was the day of the end, before he fully returned to sanity and a sense of awareness.

He had escaped bestiality, perhaps at the cost of his soul.

It was. It was, indeed. The day it would happen. He had several glimpses that day, so shocking, so brilliant in his mind, that he reaffirmed his knowledge of the coming of the event. Today it would come. Today the world would go off and burn.

One vision showed great buildings, steel and concrete, flashing like magnesium flares, burning as though they were crepe paper. The sun was raw looking, as though it might have been an eye that someone had gouged out. The sidewalks ran like butter, and charred, smoldering shapes lay in the gutters and on the rooftops. It was hideous, and it was now.

He knew his time was up.

Then the idea of the money came to him. He withdrew every cent. Every penny of the four thousand dollars; the vice president of the bank had a peculiar expression on his face, and he asked if everything was all right. Arthur answered him in epigram, and the vice president was unhappy.

All that day at the office—of course he went to work, he would not have known any other way to spend that last day of all days—he was on edge. He continually turned at his desk to stare out the window, waiting for the blood red glaze that would paint the sky. But it did not come.

Shortly after the coffee break that afternoon, he found the impression of nausea growing in him. He went to the men's room and locked himself into one of the cubicles. He sat down on the toilet with its top closed, and held his head in his hands.

A glimpse was coming to him.

Another glimpse, vaguely connected to the ones of the holocaust, but now—like a strip of film, running backward —he saw himself entering a bar.

There were words in twisting neon outside, and repeated again on the small dark-glass window. The words said: THE NITE OWL. He saw himself in his blue suit, and he knew the money was in his pocket.

There was a woman at the bar.

Her hair was faintly auburn in the dim light of the bar. She sat on the bar stool, her long legs gracefully crossed, revealing a laced edge of slip. Her face was held at an odd angle, half-up toward the concealed streamer of light over the bar mirror. He could see the dark eyes, and the heavy makeup that somehow did not detract from the sharp, unrelieved lines of her face. It was a hard face, but the lips were full, and not thinned. She was staring at nothing.

Then, as abruptly as it had come, the vision passed, and his mouth was filled with the slippery vileness of his nausea.

He got to his feet and flipped open the toilet. Then he was thoroughly sick, but not messy.

Afterwards, he went back to the office, and found the yellow pages of the phone book. He turned to "Bars" and ran his finger down the column till he came to "The Nite Owl" on Morrison and 58th Streets.

He went home especially to freshen up . . . to get into his blue suit.

She was there. The long legs in the same position, the edge of slip showing, the head at that strange angle, the hair and eyes as he had seen them.

It was almost as though he were reliving a dramatic part he had once played; he walked up to her, and slid onto the empty stool next. "May I, may I buy you a drink, Miss?"

She only acknowledged his presence and his question with a half-nod and soft grunt. He motioned to the black-tied bartender and said, "I'd like a glass of ginger ale. Give the young lady whatever she uh she wants, please."

The woman quirked an eyebrow and mumbled, "Bourbon and water, Ned." The bartender moved away. They sat silently till he returned with the drinks and Arthur had paid him.

Then the girl said, "Thanks."

Arthur nodded, and moved the glass around in its own circle of moisture. "I like ginger ale. Never really got to like alcohol, I guess. You don't mind?"

Then she turned, and stared at him. She was really quite attractive, with little lines in her neck, around her mouth and eyes. "Why the hell should I care if you drink ginger ale? You could drink goat's milk and I couldn't care less." She turned back.

Arthur hurriedly answered, "Oh, I didn't mean any offense. I was only—"

"Forget it."

"But I—"

She turned on him with vehemence. "Look, mac, you on the make, or what? You got a pitch? Come on, it's late, and I'm beat."

Now, confronted with it, Arthur found himself terrified. He wanted to cry. It wasn't the way he had thought it

would be. His throat had a choke lost in it. "I—I, why
I—"

"Oh, Jeezus, wouldn't'cha know it. A fink. My luck, always my luck." She bolted the rest of her drink and slid
off the stool. Her skirt rode up over her knees, then fell
again, as she moved toward the door.

Arthur felt panic rising in him. This was the last
chance, and it was important, how important! He spun on
the stool and called after her, "Miss—"

She stopped and turned. "Yeah?"

"I thought we might, uh, could I speak to you?"

She seemed to sense his difficulty, and a wise look came
across her features. She came back and stopped very close
to him. "What now, what is it?"

"Are you, uh, are you do, doing anything this evening?"

Her sly look became businesslike. "It'll cost you fifteen.
You got that much?"

Arthur was petrified. He could not answer. But as
though it realized the time had come for action, his hand
dipped into his jacket pocket and came up with the four
thousand dollars. Six five hundred dollar bills, crackling
and fresh. He held them out for her to see, then the hand
returned them to the pocket. The hand was the businessman, himself merely the bystander.

"Wow," she murmured, her eyes bright. "You're not as
bad as I thought, fella. You got a place?"

They went to the big, silent house, and he undressed
in the bathroom, for it was the first time, and he held a
granite chunk of fear in his chest.

When it was over, and he lay there warm and happy,
she rose from the bed and moved to his jacket. He stared
at her, and there was a strange feeling in him. He knew it
for what it was, for he had felt a distant relative to it, in
his feelings for Mother. Arthur Fulbright knew love, of a
sort, and he watched her as she fished out the bills.

"Gee," she mumbled, touching the money reverently.

"Take it," he said softly.

"What? How much?"

"All of it. It doesn't mean anything." Then he added, as
if it was the highest compliment he could summon: "You
are a good woman."

The woman held the money tightly. Four thousand dollars. What a simple little bastard. There he lay in the bed,

and with nothing to show for it. But his face held such a strange light, as though he had something very important, as though he owned the world.

She chuckled softly, standing there by the window, the faint pink glow of midnight bathing her naked, moist body, and *she* knew what counted. She held it in her hand.

The pink glow turned rosy, then red, then blood crimson.

Arthur Fulbright lay on the bed, and there was a peace deep as the ocean in him. The woman stared at the money, knowing what really counted.

The money turned to ash a scant instant before her hand did the same. Arthur Fulbright's eyes closed slowly.

While outside, the world turned so red and hot, and that was all.

*While in the US Army at Fort Knox, Kentucky, one of
my duties was Troop Information NCO, and the story
that follows (published in a magazine at that time)
seemed to me an interesting departure from the usual
stodgy troop lectures I was required to give. I read this
story to a number of groups of hardened twenty-year
men (as well as six-monthers and two-year draftees) and
asked for comment. Those who spoke up (inarticulation
is an occupational disease in the Army after a three-year
period) said it wasn't as fantastic as it sounded. That it
seemed such a thing might some day come to pass, and
they wanted to know how I, a man who had never been
in combat, had been able to devise such weird ideas, and
put them down in a form that seemed rational. I told
them I had glimpsed hell, and that I thought some day
perhaps the whole world would be that hell, unless we
stopped trying to strangle decency, unless we stopped
trying to turn logic and imagination and the hearts of
men toward a*

battlefield

SATURDAY

The first needle of the "day" came over Copernicus
Sector at 0545 . . . and seven seconds. The battery commander on White's line was an eager-beaver. His bom-
bardment cut short the coffee-pause Black's men had
planned to enjoy till at least 0550. When the hi-fi in the
ready dome screeched—a vocal transformation of the
sonorad blip indicating a projectile coming through—the
Black men looked at one another in undisguised annoyance, and banged their bulbs onto the counters.

Someone muttered, "Spoil sport!" and his companions
looked at him and laughed; obviously a repple officer,
fresh from the Academy.

One of the veterans, who had been with the outfit when
Black had been Black One and Black Two—*before* the
service merger—chuckled deep in his throat. He began to
dog down the bubble of the pressure suit. But before the

plasteel bowl was settled in place, he gibed, "Cookie-boy, you shoulda been up here when White rung in a full-blooded Cherokee named Grindbones or somethin'. You'da been on the line a'reddy at 0500. He was lobbin' 'em in solid by this time . . . had a hell of a job gettin' him croaked." He chuckled again, and several other officers nodded in remembrance.

The young lieutenant addressed as "Cookie-boy" turned an interested glance on the older man. "How did you manage to kill him? Full-day batteries at double strength? Spearhead through the craters?"

The veteran winked at his friends, and said levelly, "Nope. Easier'n that."

The young lieutenant's attention was trapped.

"Waited till he went down, and had a goon squad put a blade into his neck. Real quick. Next day, had our coffee without sweat."

The young lieutenant was still. His face gradually became a mask of disbelief and horror. "You . . . you mean you . . . oh, come *on*, you aren't *serious!*"

The veteran stared at him coldly. "Sonny, you *know* I'm serious." He dogged down the pork-bolts on his helmet. He was out of the conversation.

Yet the lieutenant continued to protest. He stood in the center of the ready dome, his helmet under his arm, his other arm thrown toward the rounded ceiling in a theatrical pose, and blurted, "But—but that's illegal! When they declared the Moon a battlefield, that was the reason, I mean, what's the sense of using up here to fight, if we still kill each other down there, I mean—"

"Oh, shut up, will you, for Christ's sake!" It was a lean, angular-faced Major with a thread-scar from a single-beam across the brutal cut of his jaw. "This wasn't war, you young clown. This was a matter of a man who fought, and stuck too closely to the rules. What you learned in the Academy was all floss and fine, man, but grow up! Use your noodle. What they taught you there doesn't always apply out here.

"When someone crosses too many wheat fields, he's bound to find a gopher hole. This Indian stepped in one of those, that's all."

The Major turned away, dogged down, and joined the rest of the line company's officers at the exitport. The young lieutenant stood alone, watching them, still muttering to himself. For with the other men on intercom only, they could not hear what he was saying:

"But the war. The—the war. They said we wouldn't chew up the Earth any more. The war . . . up here it's so much cleaner, a man can fight or die or . . . but—but they *said* they killed him on his way down.

"He was going home, to Earth, and they *killed* him—"

The Major turned with sluggish movement in the pressurized dome, and waved a metal-tooled gauntlet at the lieutenant. It was time to move to the units.

The lieutenant hurriedly dogged down, and joined the group. The veteran officer who had first spoken, turned the younger man around with rough good humor, checking the pork-bolts. Then he slapped the lieutenant on his shoulder with a comradely gesture, and they went into the exitport together.

The hi-fi had been screeching constantly for a full three minutes.

Outside, the Blacks and the Whites went into the five thousand and fifty-eighth day of the war. That particular war.

The needles came across all that early morning. In the dead black of the Darkside, their tails winked briefly as vector rockets shifted them on course. No sound broke across the airless cratered surface, but the tremors as each missile struck rang through the bowels of the dead satellite like so many gong-beaters gone mad.

Where they struck, great gouts were ripped from the grey, cadaverous dust of the surface. Brilliant flashes lived for microinstants and then were gone, for without air there could be no flames. Where the needles struck, and the face of the moon tore apart, new craters glared blindly up at space.

At 0830 on the dot, the first waves of armored units spread out from the ragged White line near Sepulchre Crater and advanced across the edge of the Darkside, into the blinding glare of the Lightside. Vision ports sphinctered down into narrow slits; filters that dimmed the blaze of light clicked over the glassene ports; men donned special equipment, and snapped switches that cut in conditioning units and coolant chambers—and turned off the feverishly working heaters.

The armored crabs came first, sliding along, hugging the contours of the moon's face, raising and lowering themselves on stalk-like plasteel rods.

The Black batteries detected their coming, but not their nature, and the first barrages were low-level missiles that zoomed silently through the glaring sunlight, passed completely over the crabs, and *shussssssed* off into the Darkside, and space, where they would circle aimlessly till the men from Ordnance Reclamation went out with their dampening nets and sucked the missiles into the cargo hatches of the ships.

But as the crabs flopped and skittered their way toward the Black line, the sonorad was able to distinguish more easily what they were. The cry went up in the tracking cells buried deep under the pumice of the moon, and new batteries were readied/launched! Doggie-interceptors screamed silently from their tubes, broke the surface of the moon like skin divers reaching water's surface, and began to follow the line of terrain, humping over rises, slipping into craters, always moving out.

The first ones made contact.

Within the crabs, the shriek of rending metal was a split microsecond ahead of the roar and flash of the doggie exploding. Great gouts of flame roared out angrily . . . and were gone as quickly, leaving in their place a twisted, bloody scrapheap where the crab had been. Another doggie struck. It caught the crab and lifted it backward and up on its stiltlegs, and then it exploded violently. Pieces of bodies were thrown two hundred feet into the airless nothing above the moon, and fell back soddenly.

All along the line the doggie's were tracking their prey and demolishing them. On the far right flank, one crab managed to train its twenty-thread on an incoming doggie, and exploded the missile before it hit. But it was a short-lived victory, for two others, coming on collision courses, zeroed in and struck simultaneously. The flash was seen fifteen miles away, the roar trembled the ground for thirty miles.

But White's offensive for the day was just beginning. In streaming waves the foot-soldiers were coming up behind the crabs. They were small pips on the sonorad units in

Black GHQ, and though they could not tell if what was coming was human or mechanical, Black continued to send out the doggies.

It was a waste of missiles; precisely what White had been counting on. The doggies homed in, and exploded, hundreds of them, each finding a lone man and atomizing him so quickly, no bit of pressure suit, weapon or flesh could be found. The missiles came down like hail, and where each struck, a man died horribly, without time to scream, with his body exploding inward in a frightful implosion of power and fire. Hundreds died all along the line, and as the doomed foot-soldiers drew the fire, the jato teams soared up from White Central and streaked before little gouts of flame, toward the Black perimeter.

Each man wore a harness over his pressure suit, with a jet unit, to drive him across the airlessness.

While their brothers died in flaming hell below them, the jato units soared through the empty sky, above the level of the terrain-skimming doggies, and dropped down like hunting falcons on the batteries.

Each man carried, in a drop-pouch, a charge of ferro-atomic explosive on a time fuse. As they whipped over the batteries, the men released their deadly cargos, directly into the barrels of the thread-disruptors, and sped up and away, back for their own lines. It was futile, of course, for sonorad had caught them, and trackbeams snaked out across the sky, picking each man off like moths caught in a flame. The jato units were snuffed out in midair, even as the ferro-atomics went off inside the disruptor barrels.

Great sheets of metal exploded outward, ripping apart the bunkers into which they had been set. The disruptors shattered their linings, throwing their own damping rods out, and in one hell's holocaust of exploding ferro-atomics, the entire battery went skyward. Three hundred men died at once, faces burned off, arms ripped loose from sockets, legs broken and shredded. Bodies cascaded from the sky and the steel ran with blood.

It was a typical day in the war.

The trackbeams probed outward, scouring the ground for landmines planted by the foot-soldiers, and exploded them on contact, then moved on. Eventually, they probed at the firm outer shell of the White perimeter.

Then the charged trackbeams of White met the Black beams, and they locked. They locked in a deadly struggle, and at opposite ends of those beams, men at control panels, in shock helmets, poured power to their beams, in a visible struggle to beat down the strength of the other.

A surge, a slight edge, a nudge of force, and White was dominant. The beam raced back the length of the weakened Black beam, and in a dome two hundred miles away, a man leaped from his bucket seat and clawed at his helmet . . . even as his eyes spouted flame, and his mouth crawed open in a ghastly scream. His charred body— burnt black inside—turned half-around, writhing, as the man beat at his dead face, and then he fell across his console.

The trackbeam was loose inside the bunker. In a matter of moments, no living thing moved in the bunker dome. But it was a double-edged weapon, for associate trackbeams of the doomed White had centered in, and now five of them joined in racing back along the Black's length. The scene in the White bunker dome was repeated. This time a woman had been under the helmet.

So it went. All day. One skirmish of foot-soldiers with ensnaring nets who stumbled across a Black detonation team, near Abulfeda Crater ended strangely, and terribly.

The detonation team was wrapped in the gooey meshes, but had barely enough time to toss their charges. The charges exploded, killing the ensnaring outfit, but also served to shatter their own helmets. They lay there for minutes, those whose helmets had merely cracked, until their air ran out, and then they strangled to death. The ones who died initially were the lucky.

At day's end, at 1630 hours, the death toll was slightly below average for a weekend. Dead: 5,886. Wounded: 4. Damages: twelve billion dollars, rounded off by the Finance & Reclamation Clerk. The batteries were silent, the crabs back in their depots and pools; the airless dead face of the moon left to the reclamation teams, who worked through the "night," preparing for Monday morning, when the war would resume.

The commuters were racked, and as the Blacks filed into their ships, as the Whites boarded theirs, the humming of great atomic motors rolled through the shining corridors of the commuters. Inside, men read newspapers and clung to the acceleration straps for the ride down.

Down to Earth.

For a quiet evening at home, and a quiet Sunday . . . before the war started again.

Almost as one, they roared free of the slight gravity, and plunged down toward the serene, carefully-tended face of the Earth. The young lieutenant hung from his strap and tried to block out the memory of what had happened that day. Not the fighting. God, that had been just fine. It had been good. The fighting. But what the older men had said. That was like saying there was no God. The moon was for war, the Earth was for peace.

They had knifed a battery sergeant on his way down? He looked about him, but all faces were turned into newspapers. He tried to put it from his mind forcefully.

Behind the commuters, the blasted, crushed and death-sprayed face of the Moon glowed in sharp relief against the black of space.

What had the Major said later:

War is good, but we have to retain our perspective.

SUNDAY

Yolande was in the kitchen dialing dinner when the chimes crooned at her. She turned from the difficult task of dictating dinner to the robochef, and wiped a stray lock of ebony hair from her forehead.

"Bill! Bill, will you answer it . . . it's probably Wayne and Lotus."

In the living room, 2/Lt. William Larkspur Donnough uncrossed his long legs, sighed as he turned off the tri-V, and yelled back softly, "Okay, hon. I'll get it."

He walked down the long pastel-tiled hall and flipped up the force screen dial, releasing the wall into nothingness. As the wall flicked out and was gone, the outside took form, and standing on Bill and Yolande Donnough's front breezeway were 2/Lt. and Mrs. Wayne M'Kuba Massaro.

"Come on in, come on in," Bill chuckled at them. "Yo's

in the kitch fixing dinner. Here, Lotus, let me have your hood."

He took the brightly-tinted hood and cape offered by the girl, a striking Melanesian with an upturned Irish nose and flaming red hair.

He accepted Wayne Massaro's service cap in the other hand and stuck the apparel to the rack, which turned into the wall, holding the clothing magnetically.

"What'll you have, Wayne, Lotus?"

Lotus raised a hand to signify none for her, but Wayne Massaro made a T with his hands. He wanted a tea-ball with a shot of herro-coke.

When Bill had jiggered the mixture together, warmed it and chilled it again, when they settled down in the formfit chairs, Donnough looked across at the other lieutenant and sighed. "Well, how'd it go your first day up there?"

Massaro frowned deeply.

Lotus broke in before her husband could answer. "Well, if you two are going to talk shop, I'm going in to see if Yo needs help." She got up, smoothed the sheath across her thighs, and walked into the kitchen.

"She'll never get used to my making the war a career," Wayne Massaro shook his head in affectionate exasperation. "She just can't understand it."

"She'll get used to it," Bill replied, sipping his own hi-skotch. "Lotus still has a lot of that Irish blood in her . . . Yo was the same way when *I* came in."

"It's so different, Bill. So very different. What they taught us in the Academy doesn't seem quite true up there. I mean—" he struggled to form the right phrase, "—it's not that they're going against doctrine . . . it's just that things aren't black and white up there—as they said they'd be when I was in the Academy—they're grey now. They don't start the morning bombardments on time, they drink coff when they should be posting, and—and—"

He stopped abruptly, and a hardness came into the set of his head. He jerked quickly, and bent to his drink. "N-nothing," he murmured, principally to himself.

Donnough looked disturbed.

"What happened, Wayne? You flinch-out when the barrage came over?"

Massaro lifted his eyes in a shocked and startled expression. "You aren't kidding, are you?"

Donnough leaned back further, and the formfit closed about him like a womb. "No, I suppose I wasn't. I know you better than that, known you too long."

There was a great deal of respect and friendship in his words. Each man sat silently, holding his drink to his lips, as a barricade to conversation for the moment. Filtered memories of shared boyhoods came to them, and talk was not right at that moment.

Then Massaro lowered the glass and said, "That jato raid came off pretty badly didn't it?" The subject had been altered.

Donnough nodded ruefully, "Yeah, wouldn't you know it. Oh, hell, it was all the fault of that gravel-brained Colonel Levinson. He didn't even send over a force battery cover. It was suicide. But then, what the hell, that's what they're paid for."

Massaro agreed silently and took a final pull at the tea-laced highball. "Uh. Good. More, daddy, more!"

Donnough waved a hand at the circle-dial of the robot bartender set into the recreation unit against the wall. "Dial away, brother frat man. I'm too comfortable to move."

A gaggle of female giggles erupted from the kitchen, and Yolande Donnough's voice came through the grille in the ceiling. "Okay you two heroes . . . dinner's on. Let's go." Then: "Bill, will you call the kids from downstairs?

"Okay, Yo."

Bill Donnough walked to the dropshaft at one corner of the living room, and slid his fingernail across the grille set into the wall beside the empty pit. Downstairs, in the lower levels of the house—sunk fifty feet into the Earth—the Donnough children heard the rasp over their own speakers, and waited for their father's words.

"Chow's on, monsters. Updecks on the double!"

The children came tumbling from their rooms and the play area, and threw themselves into the sucking force of the invisible riser-beam that lived in the dropshaft. In a second they were whisked up the shaft and stepped out in the living room:

First came Polly with her golden braids tied atop her round little head in the Swedish style. Her hands were clean. Then Bartholemew-Aaron, whose nose was running again, and whose sleeves showed it. Verushka came next, her little face frozen with tears, for Toby had bitten her calf on the way upshaft; then Toby himself, clutching his side where Verushka had kicked him in reflex.

Donnough shook his head in mock severity, and slapped Polly on the behind as he urged them to the table for dinner. "Go on you beasts, roust!"

All but Verushka, the children ran laughing to the dining hall which ran parallel to the tiled front hall of the house. Dark-haired Verushka clung to her daddy's hand and walked slowly with him. "Daddy, are you goin' to the moon tomorra'?"

"That's right, baby. Why?"

"Cause Stacy Garmonde down the block says her old ma—"

"*Father*, not old man!" he corrected her.

"—her *father's* gonna shoot you good tomorra'. He says all Blacks is bad, and he's gonna shoot you dead. Tha's what Stacy says, an' she's a big old stink!"

Donnough stopped walking and kneeled beside the wide, dark eyes. "Honey, you remember one thing, no matter what *anybody* tells you:

"Blacks are good. Whites are bad. That's the truth, sweetie. And nobody's going to kill daddy, because he's going to rip it up come tomorrow. Now do you believe that?"

She bobbled her head very quickly.

"Blacks is good, an' Whites is big stinks."

He patted her head with affection. "The grammar is lousy, baby, but the sentiment is correct. Now. Let's eat."

They went in, and the children were silent with heads only half-bowed—half staring at the hot dishes that o-popped out of the egress slot in the long table—while Donnough said the prayer:

"Dear God above, thank you for this glorious repast, and watch over these people, and insure a victory where a victory is deserved. Preserve us and our state of existence . . . Amen."

"Amen." Massaro.

"Amen." Lotus Massaro.

"Aye-men!" the children.

Then the forks went into the food, and mouths opened,

and dinner was underway. As they sat and discussed what was what, and who had gotten his, and wasn't it wonderful how the moon was the battlefield, while the Earth was saved from more destruction such as those 20th Century barbarians had dealt it.

"Listen, Bill," Massaro jabbed the fork into the air, punctuating his words, "next Sunday you and Yo and the kids come on over to *our* hovel. It'll cost *you* for a robositter next week. *We're* sick of laying out the credits."

They smiled and nodded and the dinner date for next Sunday was firmed up.

MONDAY

The commuter platforms. The ships racked one past another, pointed toward the faint light they could not see. The light of the dead battlefield. Moon. The Blacks in their regal uniforms queueing up to enter the vessels, the Whites in splendid array, about to board ship.

A Black ship lay beside a White one.

Bill Donnough boarded one as he caught a glance at the ship beside. Massaro was in line there.

"Go to hell, you White bastard!" he yelled. There was no friendliness there. No camaraderie.

"Die, you slob-creepin' Black! Drop!" he was answered.

They boarded the ships. The flight was short. Batteries opened that day—the five thousand and fifty-ninth day of the war—at 0550. Someone had chopped down the eager-beaver.

At 1149 precisely, a blindbomb with a snooper attachment was launched by 2/Lt William Larkspur Donnough, BB XO in charge of strafing and collision, which managed to worm its devious way through the White defense perimeter force screens. The blindbomb—BB—fell with a skit-course on the bunkerdome housing a firebeam control center, and exploded the dome into fragments.

Later that evening, Bill Donnough would start looking for another home to attend, the following Sunday.

Who said war was hell? It had been a good day on the line.

The pun, a sadly-misunderstood delicacy in the con-
fectionary of humor, holds for me the same kind of
infectious hilarity as a vision of three brothers named
Marx, chasing a turkey around a hotel room, or wiry
Lenny Bruce retelling his hazards and horrors on a two-
week gig in Milwaukee, or Charlie Chaplin, caught among
the gears of mechanized insanity in "Modern Times."
Humor comes packaged every which way, and profundi-
ties about its various guises and motivations do nothing
whatsoever to explain why one man's chuckle is another's
chilblain. In science fiction, with the notable exception
of the work of Kuttner, when he was wry and wacky,
the pun and humor in general have come off rather badly.
Perhaps "funny" and "science fiction" are incompatible,
or perhaps the fantasist takes himself, his Times, and
its problems too seriously. Whatever the reasons, from
time to time I have tried to make sport of the established
genres of science fantasy, as in this fable called

deal from the bottom

There was really quite a simple reason for Maxim Hirt's
presence in the death cell. He had bungled the murder
badly. The reason for his bungling was even simpler.
Maxim Hirt was awfully stupid.

He had fancied himself an actor, and for a while, had
even managed to convince a few people that such was the
case. Then came the advent of television, and he had
taken a healthy swing at appearing weekly in the homes
of the nation. The paucity of his talent was painfully apparent to anyone viewing *Clipper Ship,* his series (where-
in he played a clipper ship pilot for hire, the networks being anxious to avoid the hackneyed soldier-of-fortune for
hire theme) for a famous beer concern.

It was only after the first thirteen weeks, when signs
of sponsors on the horizon were dim, very dim, for re-
newal, that Maxim Hirt took to the telephones, to call
the critics.

"Hello, Sid?"

"Who's this?"

"Max, Sid. Old Maxie Hirt, out in Coldwater Canyon."

"Yeah, Max. What can I do ya?"

"Just wanted to call, let you know my new series, y'know *Clipper Ship*—"

"Yeah, Max, *I know.*"

"—let you know it's got a real winger comin' up this Thursday night. Filmed it down in Balboa. Real coo-coo, see it's about this broad, she's got an uncle who found a cache of diam—"

"What is it ya want, Max? A plug? So all right, so I'll give you a plug. Now . . . anything else, Max, I'm busy."

"No, no, nothing else, Sid. Just thanks a lot. I, uh, I *need* this plug, Sid."

"So okay, Maxie, okay, so take it easy. G'bye."

The review, ghosted by a writer of true action adventures for the hairy-chested men's magazines, read:

> We caught Maxim Hirt's new series *Clipper Ship* last night. Somehow we got the impression it was about a rugged, handsome guy who rents his plane and his talent to the highest bidder. Now that the light from the idiot box has faded, we don't know where we could have gotten that idea, because the paunchy, punchy bumbling of Hirt indicates no talent whatsoever. With luck, this abomination will not see renewal and Hirt can fold his tent . . .

Etcetera. The use of the word "bumbling" seemed almost mandatory when speaking of Maxim Hirt. Which was the reason, when he killed Sidney Gross, the columnist (after *Clipper Ship* folded its chocks and silently so forth), that he was apprehended. It was also the reason he managed to bungle away his lawyer's defense, and talked himself right into the death house.

Where he now sat, pad and pencil in hand, jotting down notes on what he would like for his last supper.

Maxim, being what he was, and being basically stupid, had managed to jot only one delicacy for that final repast. Baked beans.

He was sitting on the hard-tick mattress, doodling, trying to think of something else for dinner, when the air just beyond his nose shivered, shimmered and solidified into the form of a medium-sized man. The man wore a pair of tight jeans, a black turtleneck sweater and thong sandals. His beard had a definitely Mephistophalean point to it.

"Aaargh!" aaarghed Maxim as the tail which protruded from a slash in the seat of the jeans whipped across his legs.

"Oh, sorry, man," said the bearded one. "Reflex, like a shiver, every time I get summoned. Wildsville, y'know, man."

Maxim Hirt was not very bright, but he knew a devil when he saw one. Even one who looked as beat as this item. "Y-y-y-yough," Maxim pontificated.

"Oh, excuse the far out garb, daddy-cool. I just came from a set with a Tin Pan Alley song plugger. He wanted a hit, y'know. Hell, his soul ain't worth much, but then, business is business."

"I—I d-didn't summon y-y-you . . ." Maxim warbled heavily.

"Sure ya did. The doodle there," he pointed a sharp, dirty fingernail at the pad, "that's the sacred symbol, man. Like the hippest."

"But I was just d-d-doodling," Maxim argued.

"Cuts no ice, Father," said the devil. "The song plugger didn't know he was summoning, either. You'd be surprised how close to the ancient runes some of them rock n' roll lyrics get."

Maxim Hirt felt sweat coolly crawling. "What do you want from me?"

The turtled neck went up and down. "Me? Man, I don't want nothin'. I mean, like *you* invited me to the pad. What do *you* want?"

Maxim Hirt fed a bitter laugh to his lips. "There's not much you can do for me . . . by the way, do you have a name? Are you . . . are you Satan?"

The bearded one doubled with laughter, fell to the concrete floor and flopped about helplessly, his tail thrashing the walls, floor and bunk with terrible cracks. Finally he settled to rest, leaned his feet against the wall and mumbled, "Oh, man, you gas me. Satan; Satan; yet! Hell, we retired the old man aeons ago. Kicked him downstairs to a desk job. Hell, you'd never catch *him* out in the field. Thinks he's too good; shows you what a good press agent can do. Makes a personality out of a cat, next thing you know he's holding you up for elevator clauses, the whole *schlepp*."

"But who're you?" Hirt persisted. (The madness of it all hadn't really caught up with him yet.)

"Oh, man, if you *must* hang a tag, lay it on me like Skidoop. You dig?"

"Y-yes, I suppose so."

"Now, like I've made the scene, Pops, so what do you want? You name it, I frame it. Swing."

"Like I was saying," Hirt squeezed his hands together in anguish, "there isn't anything you can do for me, unless you can get me out of here. Otherwise I go to the gas chamber tomorrow morning."

Skidoop shook his head, and looked ceilingward. "No skin, man. I can do almost anything, but not that. It involves your destiny, and that's *His* bailiwick." He pointed at the ceiling. "Got the whole damned market on destinies cornered. Got there first."

"Well, then what good are you?"

Skidoop looked pained. "Man, I'm beginning to feel you are very unhip. Come to think of it, you dig Camus, Goethe, Kerouac, Rexroth, the rest of the boppers?"

"Uh . . ." Hirt began.

"I figured. You're so far out you'd have to masquerade to get back in. But like my uncle Moishe keeps tellin' me, biz is biz. So what can I do for you, right?"

"Yes. What can you do for me?"

"Well, we can always introduce an extenuating circumstance, that's cool. No rules against that; I introduce the e.c. and you change your own destiny. How's that swing?"

"Fine, but how can you do it?"

Skidoop fingered his beard, muttered something about getting a bellows and trimming it with a pair of wire cutters, and jubilantly replied, "There! You're writing down your last meal. So okay, so I give you the ability to eat. To eat and eat and eat, just keep feeding your face, without any debilitating physical side-effects, and they never gas you."

"They never gas me? Why not?"

"Who ever heard of killing a guy when he's eating his last meal? It can't be done. It's barbaric. A cincheroonie."

Maxim Hirt's commercially handsome face sloughed into an expression connoting thought. A look of guile overcame his features. "You guarantee it'll work? I can keep eating indefinitely and it won't hurt me at all?"

The bearded one waved a negligent palm. "Not a bit."

"I've heard about deals with you people," Hirt noted. "I'd have to have immortality along with it. You might fix it so I'd eat myself to death. Can you give me immortality with it?"

Skidoop thought for a moment, then said thoughtfully, "Well, we'd have to put in a clause about that. Contingent on whether or not they avoid frying you. If they don't, you get the immortality. But if they do, why should I waste valuable life-force on you, since *His* destiny ruling would come first, anyhow, and they'd gas you anyway."

"I get immortality if this extenuating circumstance works, right?"

"Correct-o-roony," said Skidoop, snapping his fingers in contrapuntal variation.

Hirt again looked wary. "What do you get? I've heard about how you guys always gyp a client."

"The vicissitudes of a bad press, man. Nothin' but a hard sell from *Him*. We wouldn't stay in business long if we didn't give good service."

"What do you get, then?"

"Your soul, man, the standard kick."

Hirt went white, and shook his head from side-to-side with frantic intensity. "Uh-uh, uh-uh, uh-uh!" he voted the motion down.

Skidoop spread his hands. "Oh, man, will you like please cool it. I mean, fade blade. You know what your soul is?"

Hirt waggled his head again.

"It's only your imagination. That's all. I mean, they jabber about this and that and the soul kick and the life force kick, and all of it, when the straight poop is that it's only your imagination."

"That's all?"

"That's all, daddy-cool. And let's face it, if I wasn't bound by the Fair Trade Union, I wouldn't even have come on this summons. I mean, let's face it, dad, you haven't got much imagination to begin with."

"And nothing else?"

"Nothing else."

"Honest Injun?"

"Tear out my heart and hope to burn!"

"Okay, it's a deal. But let's get it straight once more . . ."

"I'll run through it, from the top: I give you the ability to keep eating, as long as you live, and if they don't gas you, then you get immortality on top of it. In exchange for which all I take is your imagination."

"Where's the pen to sign the paper?" Hirt asked, now anxious.

"Paper, pen? Oh, man, all them modern fantasy writers been corrupting the legend again. We do it in blood; good old legal tender. No contract, just a mix of the haemoglobin, tom."

Hirt was surprised.

"What type are you, man, so I'll know if I have to ring in a notary with all-purpose corpuscles? CPA, Corpuscle Public Accountant."

Hirt tried to remember, then said, "I'm type 'O'."

"Nutsville," Skidoop caroled, and bit a hole in his wrist. The blood began spurting. He offered a finger to Hirt, and the condemned man used the sharp fingernail to start a scratch on his own forearm. They mixed.

"Done!" Skidoop chortled, grabbed the imagination in both hands, wrenched it loose, and split the scene.

Maxim Hirt sat on the bunk, and knew all would be well. He had it knocked.

Which was true. Because when they brought him his meal, he ate and ate and ate and ate.

And did not stop eating; so they commuted his sentence to life, because you can't strap a man in the gas chamber who hasn't finished his last meal.

Which would not have been such a bad way to finish out a life, sitting there eating all day and night, except that when Skidoop took Hirt's imagination, he took Hirt's ability to think of anything else but baked beans to eat.

So the last meal consisted of baked beans, plate by plate by plate by . . .

Obviously, it was a deal from the bottom.

In many ways, it was a fate *worse* than death.

Since I was thirteen, to greater or lesser degree, I have been a rootless person. Oh, there have been homes and residences and all the trappings of being settled, but aside from my days in New York, which always seem to me to be the best days, I've wandered. Up and down and back across the United States, wherever the vagaries of life have carried me with my writing, military service, marriage, job opportunities or just plain chance. And from these peregrinations has come the belief that not only is home where the heart is, but the heart is undeniably where the home is. I was also prompted by this obscure notion, to write

the wind beyond the mountains

It is down in the Book of the Ancestors with truth. The Ruskind know but one home. Ruska is home, for home shall be where the heart is. The stars are not for the Ruskind, for they know, too, that the heart is where the home is.

Wummel saw the shining thing come down. He watched it from the stand of gnarl-bushes as the pointed thing flamed across the sky, streaking toward the red sun. It flashed brightly above the land, and disappeared quickly. Wummel found himself shaking.

His pointed face quivered, and his split tongue slipped in and out of his mouth nervously. It had not been a bird, *that* was obvious. Nor a beast of the land. Whatever it had been, it stirred a strange sensation in him.

As though he were seeing a long-missing brother returning from across the mountain passes, coming home finally, after a long, long absence. But that could not be: this metal thing he had never seen before. Yet he could not shake the feeling.

Wummel, for the first time in a life filled with fears, was terribly frightened.

He crouched down, his triply-jointed legs crossing under him. He crouched down to watch the sky. If the flaming thing was to make another appearance, he would be there when it did.

He had not long to wait. The sun had slipped across the pale blotch of grey sky, when the thing appeared again. The thing dipped as it approached The Forest, and banked down toward the rising yellow-feathertops of the trees. In a few moments Wummel saw the falling thing point its sharp beak into the trees, and disappear through the foliage.

A muted roaring came to Wummel's horn-bell ears, and a ropey pillar of angry smoke twisted up into the late afternoon sky.

The roaring grew in violence, then suddenly ceased. The semi-silence of The Forest dropped down again, as though it had never been shattered.

The *swip-swip-swip* of the forest crickets resumed. The cough and growl of the land beasts took up where it had died. A yellow-striped prowl-cat slipped through the trees at the edge of the clearing. The wind whistled softly in among the yellow feather-leaves, and The Forest looked as it had always looked.

Only Wummel, of all the Ruskind, knew the thing had come, knew The Forest was not as it had always been.

And he turned immediately, scuttling off on digger fingers and triple-jointed legs, to tell the Ruskind. He might have sent the message by thought to the One, who would have told the Ruskind, but—somehow—this message had to be delivered personally. He disappeared through the undergrowth.

In The Forest, there was movement from the thing that had ceased to flame.

"Sellers, dispatch your crew into that section of the forest over there. See if you can find anything of the creatures who built that village.

"Galen, I'd like you to take the flit—be careful now— and check if those mountains we saw are inhabited. Let's make this a thorough one, boys. It's the last one before home."

He fitted the picture of a spaceman. Tall, bronzed from

many suns; wide and blocky hands, altogether able hands that commanded with ease.

Eyes blue as the seas over which he had flown, a mouth that spoke sharply, but bore no grudge. A man with lines of character in his face; not a blank mold of a face that smiled and made sounds, but a face that had been the home of sadness and hard times. A man who had grown tired but never beaten, searching for an ideal.

"This survey has to be *really* good, Charlie," the Captain said to his First. "There's talk back home about too much for appropriations for the Mapping Command. They may swallow us into the mercantile guild systems. That wouldn't be so hot." He spoke earnestly, and there was a depth to his words.

The First Mate wanted badly to touch this man, to lay a hand on his arm and say, "We'll make it, Vern," or something less trite. But he could not. Instead, he remarked, "You look tired, Vern. Catch much during the last leg?"

The Captain shook his head and grinned broadly, though the weariness was moving in his eyes. "You know me, Charlie. 'No-Wink, No-Blink, No-Nod Kovasic' they called me at the Academy." Then, the jibe still moist on his lips, he sobered.

"Bring something back, Charlie. Bring it back—we need it bad. We need something to open their eyes back home. To make them understand we're not just idly flitting around the galaxy—that we can bring back useful information. We have to keep the Command in business. It was thirty years coming, Charlie—be a hell of a note to lose it now.

"We need it, Charlie." He added softly, almost to himself, as he turned away, "Need it bad."

They came clumping through The Forest, nineteen of them, walking strangely.

They moved erect, with their hands swinging at their sides. Their hands were even different. How could they dig without spade-shaped fingers? How could they hear from those odd little flat things so close to their heads?

Their eyes. Such strange eyes. Mere, angry slits.

The eyes watching the strange ones were not slits. They were huge, platter-like organs without lids. They watched unblinking as the strangers from the flaming thing tromped through The Forest.

They were going to the Village Home.

The thought went out from the One, to the other Ruskind, *Be careful, my children. They seem to bode no harm, but they are not of Ruska, they are not the Ruskind; not of the land, nor of the sea, nor of the air we know. Be careful.*

Wummel heard the thought, and hunkered deeper under the spread roots of the gnarl-bush. Yet . . . there was something about these strange erect wanderers that drew him.

Is it because I saw them first? he wondered. Or is it something else. I feel—I sense—a deeper bond in these strange ones. They are not wholly unknown to me.

He reached out daintily, searching with his mind, plucking delicately as though on some fragile musical instrument.

A stirring of buried racial memory. A common germ, a flame, a whirling nebula and a throwing-out of flashing arms. One parent. One world, so far back even the concept had been drowned by memory on memory.

He watched their progress, deeper into the mingled tree-shapes. The Forest held many of Wummel's people. The Ruskind had left the Village Home, till the strange ones left the planet.

His eager eyes caught the every flicker of their bodies, the every tread of their step, the every thought of their minds. A wild, conflicted and confused something, as rolled and entwined as the slender stringer arms of the sewlan vines. Their minds were never at rest. They could not speak between each other—in thoughts—and they struggled in the cages of their bodies to communicate.

Occasionally one would move its mouth at the other, and a fraction of the real communication would be understood.

There was a wandering in them. They were never at rest. Their lives were meshes of step and run and scamper. Never at peace, never at rest, always driven on, always driven on . . .

Father, the thought blossomed. *I want to follow them, I want to listen more to them.*

Thought returned: *Be careful, my son.*

They caught him in the village. They had been studying the thatchy hutches, when the First Mate had seen him. He had been watching them from the edge of the forest, and the First caught the movement of his green fur from the corner of his eye.

He had dispatched men to circle the thing, and they had closed in on it carefully. It had started to scamper away when they were a good twenty feet from it. But the enmeshing action of the power-driven elasticord in their Molasses-guns had trapped it.

The little thing lay still, as they picked him up, warped into a small furry ball, with the adhesive elasticord wound about him in many twistings. They carried him out of the forest, and laid him before the First Mate.

It lay still even as they surrounded him. It stared up out of saucer-sized yellow eyes, and the green smooth fur of its flanks quivered under their gaze.

"Is it animal, vegetable, or . . ." one of the noncoms began, but the First Mate cut him off with a wave of the hand.

"Do you feel anything?"

The others shook their heads, but the First noticed one man whose eyes had clouded, whose brow was furrowed with lines of concentration. As though he were listening for a sound, far off.

"Queer lookin' little thing," one of the men said. "Wonder what it eats. Or if *we* can eat *it!*" He began to chuckle.

The First cut him off hard.

"Shut up!" His face had an odd shine to it, as though a thin film of perspiration was about to break through.

"I—I—" the words only half-formed.

He knew what he wanted to say, but he could not. The thing before him was a beast of the woods; a dumb thing with neither mind nor manner. Still . . . he was certain it was—he could hardly form the thought—*speaking to him!*

Strange words with a strange tone. Words and thoughts of a million years. The thoughts of an entire race; a race that had never left its world, that had never climbed from the dirt, and yet was sublimely happy. Tied to its world, and at peace with the universe.

The First Mate had been in space eighteen years. He had grown hard fighting for the Mapping Command, and it had been many more years than he could remember since he had cried.

But he felt the tears beginning. The thoughts were too sweet, too clear, too demanding in their picturing.

"Take him to the ship," he said, turning toward the forest. "We'll let the Captain have a look at him."

The men lifted the little beast and carried him back through the foliage.

The First Mate followed a few feet behind, his head lowered.

They wanted to take Wummel to Earth.

He could hear them saying it in the caverns of their minds. The thought came strongest from the man they called the Captain. He thought, and the thoughts came to Wummel, and Wummel listened, but he could *only* listen at first.

To Earth, the thought said. *To Earth, and the Command is saved. And the wandering won't be stopped, and we can go off across the Rim and find the last planet ever. Then we can come back. But till they find the last planet, there will be movement.*

These were thoughts lower than thoughts. They were buried deeper, deeper than the fibers knew they reached. Buried down where this Captain could never really see them, only feel the burning of their message in his legs. And he moved, always moved—without rest.

Constantly driven on, with no sleep, with no rest, no ending. Wummel felt the heart in him go out to these strange beasts of the eternally nighted sky. They were terrible in their everlasting wandering. Even the home world was to them merely a base to which they could return occasionally.

Now they wanted to take him from *his* home.

Wummel considered it, the chill spreading up from his spine. He knew he was as deeply rooted to Ruska as the sewlan or the gnarl-bushes. Could it be conceivable that he might go, and never return?

Wummel found it difficult to live on his world, sometimes. The land beasts were huge, hungry and fearsome. The prowl-cats and the sytazill were always on the hunt, and Wummel's people had never quite learned to avoid them. For the land beasts were not precisely ignorant brutes. They had minds, and souls, Wummel imagined, and their actions could not always be predicted. It was better that way.

Then too, there was the sucking valley, where the mud ran up over the walls of the canyon and dragged down those unlucky enough to be blown there during the Time of Winds. There were many things that made life hard for the Ruskind. But it was good, too.

It was good when the triple moons rose in blue and fire-red and white. Then the coolness came. When the long magenta blossoms of the aloo broke forth and shot many feet into the air, showering all the hills till they were carpeted bright and happy with the color. And most of all, Wummel loved the sighing, whispering, chortling winds that blew to him from beyond the mountains. He had often wanted to go there, beyond the stark black mountains, and see the Wind Lord who made the happy puffs that became the wind.

They wanted to take him from that, all that, and send him hurtling through a black and a dead and a night so deep that no man and no Ruskinda would ever see to its far end.

He knew of the stars. He had seen them. His people spoke of them. But not to go there. Never that!

They wanted to make a wanderer of him. They wanted him for show and study on their own base world, their Earth.

They wanted to cast him from his home and set him— as *they* did—wandering on that star-road that never ended, but twisted and wound in among the eternal graves of the beings that had wandered to their deaths.

The tears, thick and oily, started to Wummel's eyes, even as the Earthmen let the big plug-door sigh shut, blocking away the light of Ruska. And the bolts thrust home.

Then he felt the shivering, and the roaring, and the hungry urgency of the metal itself, as the ship pleaded to the men, thundered its desire to go. Go, and never return. Never stop again on this world of the three moons and the blue, blue seas, and the razor-toothed mountains, and the winds blowing from beyond those mountains. Never come again. And never!

The takeoff was a sloppy one. Somehow the tapes had been fed in with a bit too much fervency, as though the Drivemaster had wanted away from the tiny world.

Captain Kovasic stood with his back to the little cage. He stood watching through the viewport as the multi-colored world dropped away under them, till it was a picture drawn on a blackboard.

He felt the thoughts bubbling up in him, and he turned, reluctantly.

He stared at the little green creature, huddled into a ball, its huge eyes staring. The creature was shivering, mocking the quivers of the ship itself. Kovasic felt that had the being possessed eyelids, it would surely have had them screwed tightly, painfully shut.

The thoughts roiled and swirled, like dirty oil on an angry sea, and he felt the rising of his own longing in his throat. A longing he had never actually known he possessed.

He knew, with a startling burst of clarity, the writing in the Book of the Ancestors. He knew of the Ruskind and of the roots that grow deeper, far deeper, than the mere roots of race. He knew he was a wanderer, that all his people were wanderers, and how they would end. He knew, too, what he had done to Wummel.

He watched as the little creature's golden eyes frosted over, and its fur ceased quivering.

The First Mate had not wanted to come to the bridge. He had known the creature was there, and he had not relished the ideas and disturbing thoughts the being seemed to create.

But he came, because he knew the progress report must be delivered. At all times the Captain must know how far they had come, how fast they were going, how soon they would arrive.

All the information of running.

When he stepped onto the bridge, he saw only the Captain's back, and the blind, blank black face of the viewport. The Captain had deaded it. Space was cut off for the first time since the ship had been launched.

"Captain . . . ?" His voice was a softness, as though all the fragile glass and spiderweb of the silence hanging between them might shatter.

"It died," Kovasic said, staring straight ahead into no-where.

"Died? The specimen? How? What could have . . . ?"

"It couldn't live away from the planet. We broke its heart. It's that simple; laugh if you want—breaking its heart—but it died, that's all. And now we'll go home. Home." He said the last word with an odd, thick sound. As though it had been something he had known so very long age, and forgotten, and substituted another meaning for it, and now suddenly had learned what it was again, and knew he was damned because it was beyond him forever.

"The Command. It'll be—it'll get swallowed by the mercantile . . ." The First began, fumblingly.

The Captain whirled, his face half-angry, half-imploring.

"Don't you understand, Charlie? Don't you know? You ran away from the creature, you must have heard what it said.

"Don't you see? The Command, the mercantile guilds, Earth, the searching, the always hungering for more more more more . . ."

He ground to a stop, as though it all meant what he said it meant. Empty nothing.

Then he said the one thing that *did* matter. He said it knowing he was sounding the one truth that was inescapable. The one truth that Wummel had died because he knew had been deprived him:

"There is no home, if there is no rest. There is no rest if there is no *Home*."

Then he turned back to the viewport. The First Mate moved to leave, but the soft words of the Captain, spoken against the deaded surface, stopped all movement. Staring at the empty surface, he murmured.

"It died, and the last thing it felt . . ." he paused.

"It pitied us, Charlie. That's all. It didn't hate us for killing it.

"It just pitied us."

In the original edition of ELLISON WONDERLAND, this space was occupied by a short story appearing under the title, "The Forces that Crush." Some years later I rewrote it, included it in my collection THE BEAST THAT SHOUTED LOVE AT THE HEART OF THE WORLD (Signet Books, 1974), and it appeared under the title Paul Fairman gave it when he published it in Amazing Stories back in the fifties: "Are You Listening?" I didn't want to let it appear twice so soon, so I've pulled out of obscurity a nice little fable about a robot that I've always liked. Now, if it weren't that my old friend Isaac Asimov has written just about everything there is to write about robots (and what Ike didn't do, Kuttner did as Lewis Padgett), I would have no trepidations, but Ike and I have been gigging each other with love and truculence for almost twenty-five years, and I just know he'll have some smartass remarks to make the next time I see him, when, with twinkle in eye, he finds some circumlocutious way to compare his famous robotics stories with my humble, yet undeniably brilliant, effort called

back to the drawing boards

Perhaps it was inevitable, and perhaps it was only a natural result of the twisted eugenics that produced Leon Packett. In either case, the invention of the perambulating vid-robot came about, and nothing has been at all the same since.

The inevitability factor was a result of live tri-vid, and the insatiable appetite for novelty of the vid audience. If vid broadcasts came from Bermuda in tri-vid color with feelie and whiff, then they wanted wide-band transmission from the heart of the Sudetenland. If they got that, it wasn't enough; next they wanted programs from the top of Everest. And when they had accomplished that—God only knows how—the voracious idiot mind of the audiences demanded more. They demanded live casts from the Millstone, circling above the Earth; then it was Lunar fantasies with authentic settings . . . and Mars . . . and Venus . . . and the Outer Cold Ones.

Finally, Leon Packett stumbled upon the secret of a perfect, self-contained tri-vid camera, operating off a minute force-bead generator; and in his warped way, he struck instantly to the truth of the problem—that the only camera that could penetrate to those inner niches of the universe that the eyes of man demanded to glimpse, was a man himself.

How completely simple it was. The only gatherer of facts as seen by the eyes of a man . . . were the eyes of a man. But since no man would volunteer to have his head sliced open, his brains scooped out, and a tri-vid camera inserted, Leon Packett invented Walkaway.

In all due to the devil, it was coldly logical, and it was a beautiful bit of workmanship. Walkaway had the form of a human being, even to ball-and-socket joints at the knees and elbows. He stood just under seven feet tall, and his hide was a burnished permanodized alumasteel suit. His hands could be screwed off, and in their stead could be inserted any one of three dozen "duty" hands, withdrawn from storage crypts, located in the limbs. His head was the only part of him that was slightly more than human. Brilliantly so, again offering Satan his plaudits.

Where the center of the face on a human would have been, the revolving lens wheel with its five turrets bulked strangely. Beneath the lens wheel a full-range audio grid lay with criss-crossed strangeness. The audio pickups were located on either side, as well as front and rear, of the head.

Two sets of controls were used on Walkaway. One set was imbedded in the right arm (and would snap up at the proper coded pressing of a lock-snit at the wrist) and was chiefly used by Walkaway himself when he was asked to play back what he had heard or seen.

The other console controls were in the back, and to my knowledge, were never employed after Walkaway's initial test runs. He disliked being pawed.

Naturally, the dissenters at Walkaway's birth, who declaimed the sanity of giving a robot volition and "conscience" with as much strength as his metal frame held, were shouted down. The creature—well, wasn't he?—had to have the right of free choice, if he was going to get the story in all its fullness and with a modicum of imagination, which the vid audience demanded.

So Walkaway was made more human.

He was able to disagree, to be surprised, to follow instructions *almost* as they were given, and to select the viewing subjects he wished, when he was filming. Walkaway was a most remarkable . . . what?

Creature.

"Leon, you've *got* to do it. Don't be obstinate, that's just being foolish. They'll get him somehow, Leon!"

Leon Packett spun in the chair, facing the window. His back was very straight, and his neck held a rigid aloofness. "Get out, McCollum. Get out and tell your ponysoldiers to do the same. Leave me alone!"

Alan McCollum threw up his hands in eloquent frustration. "Lee, I'm trying to get *through* to you, for God's sake! All I ask is you listen to them, and *then* make a decision—"

Packett spun in the chair. His feet hit the floor with a resounding clump and he leaned one elbowed arm at McCollum. His index finger was an unwavering spear, the tip of which aimed between McCollum's sensitive dark brown eyes.

"Now look, McCollum. I spent fifteen years in a cellar lab, working what I could, and experimenting as best I could, soldering old pieces together because I couldn't get a Frericks Grant. Then I happened to think of putting two old gadgets together, and I came up with a miracle. Now I'm big time, and the Frericks Foundation uses me in their institutional advertisements."

His lean, horsey face was becoming ruby-blotched.

"But Walkaway is *mine*, McCollum! Mine! I dreamed him up and I sweated constructing him. I starved for fifteen years, McCollum. Fifteen. You know how long that is? While you and all your MIT buddies were piddling around putting chrome on old discoveries, I was missing all the good things."

McCollum's jaws worked. His eyes dulled with suppressed fury. "That isn't fair, Lee. You almost enjoy your misery, and you *know* it."

Packett stood up. His face was a crimson and milk patchwork. "Get out!" he snarled. His thin lips worked loosely, and his nostrils flared. "Get out and leave me alone. Walkaway is *not* going to Carina. Not Epsilon Carinae, not Miaplacidus, nowhere in Carina. Walkaway is staying here, where I can keep getting my commissions, where I can guarantee my future. It's been too dirty for me to start being patriotic now, McCollum, so you can trot out there and tell your Space Patrol buddies I'm not in the market."

McCollum was about to shout an answer, but he stood up instead. Stood up and stared at the contorted features of Leon Packett.

He turned and took three steps to the slidoor. With his palm—but not fingertips—fitted into the depression, he paused, and looked back at Packett. "There are doctors who can help you, Leon."

"Get out, you sonofabitch!"

A heavy plastex ashtray crashed into the wall beside McCollum's head. His fingertips touched and the door slid.

Perhaps he knew it was inevitable. The machinery he had always despised, now ground its wishes out in the dust of his ambitions. He had suffered by his own hand, and had cursed the powers that had overlooked him. But now they wanted his vid-robot, his Walkaway. He knew they would reimburse him handsomely, but that was not what he sought.

Packett knew, and he moved to preserve his will, despite the loss of his invention. Late into the night he worked, on the smallest, most unnoticeable alterations in the printed circuitry of Walkaway's "mind" and "conscience". Late into the night on a space of plastex no larger than the surface of an eyeball. And when he fell into an exhausted sleep, as the daylight ribboned across the laboratory walls, Walkaway stood as he had stood.

Unchanged.
Apparently.
But changed.
Inwardly.

He managed to salvage his old age. By the simple expedient of refusing to allow ownership to switch from his hands—and after his death the hands of the Frericks Foundation—into the hands of the military, he preserved a hold on Walkaway. The Guard—his terminology "Space Patrol" had long since been aborted, despite the tabloid's efforts to keep it alive—were forced to hire Walkaway. They signed him on as a civilian employee, paid a monthly wage, a per diem remuneration, as well as travel expenses.

The wages were to be paid on demand, and books were kept by the Frericks Foundation, whose interest in Packett and Walkaway were more than merely scientific. With the world-famous Leon Packett associated with them, there could be no doubt about doles and grants. The Frericks Foundation had men at its helm whose interests penetrated into other fields than scientific: politics, finance, authority. The men were exceedingly careful to keep books.

The Guard's first enterprise in which Walkaway figured prominently was the remote from Bounce Point.

Bounce Point was the super-satellite constructed out beyond Pluto. It had been thrown up as the last outpost of Solar enterprise. Man's final touch with what was known, before he leaped off into the unknown.

From Bounce Point, great and silver and ebony in Pluto's sky, Walkaway was destined to begin the long ride out.

McCollum and his contemporaries had not been idle. While Leon Packett nursed his hatred of Authority and the Machine of Empire, they had been hard at work. The warp-drive was ready. Nuzzling the gleaming inner hull of its drive chamber, the warp-drive was larger than later models would surely have to be. It was a giant nest of power units, small inside larger, larger inside still larger, and finally, resting in a brace-socket at the tip of the final unit, a force-bead of incalculable power. That was the random factor. How hard could the warp-drive be pushed by this force-bead?

What were the effects on a man, sent through not-space?

For the test, what better guinea pig than a metal man with a camera face. In tri-vid, with audio pickup, what better record could be offered for study.

The initial flight of W-1 to Carina, lost in the star heaps of space, would be accomplished with no human hand at the controls. The robot would take the bounce.

Leon Packett lay on a dirty bunk in a haven back of the

CentralPort space pads. The room was a flop, with the tackboard walls only stretching halfway to the ceiling. The other half of the wall was strand-wire, put in to offer a slight deterrent to thieves in the other cubicles, in no way to offer privacy. Packett lay on the bunk, a half-emptied bottle of Paizley's rigid between his side and his arm, held upright by his armpit. His long, almost oriental eyes were closed in stupor, and his horsey face was a Madame Toussoud wax reproduction. His breathing was irregular . . .

. . . when McCollum found him.

"Packett!" All civility was gone. There are worse things than insults. The insults had not alienated McCollum. The others had. "Packett! They want you. Get out, Packett!"

He dragged the bottle with its sour smell from Leon Packett's armpit, and threw it to the floor. Where the wrench of the bottle had not disturbed the drunken man, where McCollum's shot-like shouts had not roused him, the soft gurgling emptying of the bottle succeeded.

Packett came straight up on the bunk, hands in his wild hair, and he screamed. With eyes closed, with deep lined areas about the sockets, he shrieked. *"Let me alone!"*

Then he opened his eyes.

After he had sobbed, and dry-heaved, McCollum got him to his feet, and out of the filthy, wino-odored cubicle. There was a small argument about three days rent, with a ferret-like man behind the cage, but McCollum flashed over a five-note and they went into the street. Where the sounds of traffic overhead on the expressways deafened Packett, rising over him, like the spread, leathery wings of a pterodactyl, and dropped over him with suffocating strength. He tried to bolt back into the building.

McCollum was forced to hit him.

The hack ride was uneventful.

The Frericks Foundation rose alabaster on the third tier of the New Portion. McCollum would have paused to clean Leon Packett's face and innards, had not the Guard representatives spotted them as they left the hack at tier level. The gay uniforms of the Guard were ranked in the hall as McCollum steadied his sodden cargo into the building.

"My God, purulent!" one Guardsman snorted sourly.

"Is that Packett?" a dapper, balding Guardsman asked. His shoulders bore Commander boards. McCollum nodded. He tried to move past with Packett.

The Commander stopped them. McCollum explained, "He was on the Strip. He's not been well."

"Don't cover for him, McCollum. He's a waste, and there should be no glossing. The man is a waste. Can he talk?"

McCollum shrugged, still supporting Packett, whose legs were taffy. "I suppose. I don't know how much coherence you'll get out of him, but I suppose he can talk."

The Commander nudged a thumb toward a conference room. "Bring him along."

They started toward the room, and Packett began to blather. Even as they thrust him into a chair, his words fumbled and roiled. "They with power . . . laws and can't do, and do, and have this with what they let you do. *I* know! I've *al*ways known! The wheels with grinding down and they are afraid, so they rule you . . . rule . . ."

He went on ramblingly, almost semi-conscious, his words—more, his accents—tirades against authority and government. They had hampered him, but he would get even.

The Guard listened closely, for after all, this *was* Packett, the inventor of Walkaway. They listened, and finally, the Commander put his gloved hand, his crimson gloved hand, across Packett's mouth. "That will be enough, man," he deep-throated, with suppressed fury.

"Tell him what we want, McCollum," the esoteric purulent-caller urged the Frericks man.

McCollum's eyebrows went up and his lips thinned with resignation. The military never *could* pull its weight in these matters. "Leon," McCollum said, slipping to one knee beside Packett's chair. "Leon, they want to take Walkaway back to the drawing boards. They think he has too much initiative. Leon? Can you understand—"

"No!

"No, by God, damn their eyes, *no!* Not a touch. Not a wire. Nothing! He stays as he is! If they want to use him, damn them they've robbed me of my fortune, now they'd pick my brain work apart, no I say!"

They argued and pleaded and cajoled and screeched at

him for the better part of five hours. But he was firm. He still owned Walkaway. The Frericks Foundation employed Packett by grant, but Walkaway was still his own, and when it came down to it, not a military personnel at all. Walkaway was a free entity. A bond slave of metal set free. If they wanted him to go to Carina—as Packett had resolved it to himself—he would go as he was now, today, now.

So the Guard had to accept it that way. They had to take Walkaway with his individuality . . . too much for a robot? And they had to send him on the first bounce to the stars, as a metal man with thoughts of his own.

That was as it should have been.

For had not Leon Packett created Walkaway?

Had not Packett re-arranged the circuits to provide a hidden factor the Guard knew nothing about?

Had it not all been planned that way?

To results we know now.

The ship was crazily-shaped. It was a sundial. With a thick trunk, and two clear face-plates at either end. Great face plates of clear substance, through which Walkaway could train his turret eyes, and see the universe as it whirled by in not-space. The drive apertures were set at angles around the thick trunk of the ship, and there were no sleeping compartments, no galley, no chairs, nothing a metal servant would find useless.

The ship W-1 blasted free of Bounce Point on March 24th, 2111, its sole occupant a robot named Walkaway, whose face was a triple-turret tri-vid camera, and whose mind was the mind of a metal man with initiative. A certain initiative that only one man knew existed.

The ship left on March 24th. On March 31st, Leon Packett gripped a pair of heavy scissors and thrust them deep into his neck.

His will was a masterpiece of maudlin self-pity; but it released Walkaway from all human obligations, setting him *in toto* free. He was a singular now. Not an invention, but a civilian employee of the military Guard. He was to receive payment per diem for his work, and his accounts were to be handled by the Frericks Foundation.

Whatever Walkaway earned, remained his own.

The ship went out on March 24th 2111.

It returned three hundred and sixty-five years later. And the future began.

Oh, Lord! The records were covered with dust. But valid, that was the rub. The Frericks Foundation had sunk in its own mismanagement, and a pleasure sanctuary had risen on its whited bones. The New Portion was now called the Underside, for tiers had risen high on high to the fiftieth level above that tier. Now there was a planet-wide government, and the ship W-1 had become a legend. The robot Walkaway had become a myth. The ship had never been heard from again, and as will happen, with all cultures, time had passed the concept of star travel by.

There was a broken-nosed statue of Leon Packett on the third tier, many miles from where the Frericks Foundation had stood. A statue that called him one of the great inventors of all time and all Mankind. There were no scissors in the statue.

When the ship came down past the Moon, and its warning gear telemetered out the recog-signals, the Earth Central control tower was lost in disbelief. A sloe-eyed brunette who was in charge of deciphering and matching recog-signals with the call letters of those ships out, called for a checker. Her section chief, a woman who had been on the job for eighteen years, matched the recog-signals, and turned to the younger girl with a word lost on her lips.

The call went in to Guard Central immediately.

They denied landing co-ordinates to the W-1 and held it aspace till they had found the records in the sub-cellar of the pleasure sanctuary on the third level. When they had the files, they knew the story completely, and they sent word to berth-in the W-1.

Walkaway looked the same.

Huge and graceful, his face vaguely human, his body a sort of homo sapiens plus, he slid down a nylex rope from the cargo aperture of the sundial-shaped ship. He had not bothered to lower the landing ramp. As he came down the single strand, his metallic reflection shone in the smooth landing-jack's surface. The reflection of Walkaway shone down and down and over again down as he slid quickly to the pad.

They watched, as they might watch a legend materialíze. This was the fabled robot that had gone out to seek the stars in Carina, and had returned. Three hundred and sixty-five years the W-1 had been away, and now it had returned. What would the vid-cameras of this perambulating robot show? What wonders awaited man, now that his interest was roused in the immensities of space? The Guard watched, ranked around the pad, as Walkaway slid down the nylex rope. The great sundial-shaped ship held high above them—unlike any other of the sleek vessels in the yard—tripod poised on its high-reaching legs.

Then the robot touched Earth, and a shout went up.

Home is the hunter, home from the hill . . .

Three hundred and sixty-five years. No one was left who remembered this creature of flawless metal. No one who had seen Walkaway go out on the shuttle to Bounce Point.

Bounce Point that was itself two hundred years dust. Gone in the struggle for the Outer Cold Ones.

The robot came across the pad, his shining feet bright against the blackened pad-rock, and his close-up turret ground near-to-silently away, taking in the reception ceremony for posterity.

Before the Guard representative could issue forth with the practiced phrases of a hundred other receptions, the robot said clearly, "It is good to be back. Where is Leon Packett?"

How strange it was—they said later—a legend stood asking them about another legend. Paul Bunyan inquiring after Zeus. What could they say? Few of them even knew of the man named Leon Packett. Those who knew, were vague where he was concerned. After all, three hundred and sixty-five years. The Earth had changed.

"I asked: where is Leon Packett? Which of you is from the Frericks Foundation?"

There were no answers. And then someone in the front ranks of the Guard, someone who knew his history, said: "You have been gone three hundred years and more, robot."

"Leon Packett . . . ?"

"Is dead," finished the Guardsman. "Long dead. Where have you been so long?"

And a circuit closed as data was fed to Walkaway.
And the future was assured.

Loneliness. Leon Packett had done his work well. The attempts to take Walkaway back to the drawing boards would have shown them what Packett had done. He had freed the robot's soul completely. Not only legally, but in actuality. Walkaway felt great sadness. There had only been one other who knew his inner feelings. That had been Leon Packett. There had been empathy between them. The man a bit mad, the robot a bit man. They had spent evenings together, as two childhood friends might have; the man and the faceless metal creature, product of the man's mind. They had not talked much, but a word had brought understanding of concepts, of emotions:

"All of them."

The robot immobile, answering metallically, "Power."

"Someday, someday . . ."

"Checks."

"Balances."

"Oh, Walkaway. Someday, just someday!"

"I know."

The nights had passed restlessly for Packett, while the sickness within him festered. The robot had been constructed in the image of the man. Seeing everything through its vid-eyes, hearing everything through its pickups, but saying little, working hard. Then Packett had known he would die, and Walkaway would live on. An extension of himself; the sword he would someday wield.

He had worked long into the night, foreseeing where others would not foresee, could not foresee, though they had the knowledge. For Leon Packett had been gifted. Sick, but gifted, and he had left his curse, left his justice, left his vengeance, to live on after he was gone.

Walkaway learned of Leon Packett's death, and the circuit Packett had tampered with, that he had wanted to close at the knowledge of his death, snapped to with a mental thud that only Walkaway felt, that the universe was soon to know.

The robot turned to the Guardsmen and made the one request no one would have considered, the one request that was his legally to make:

"Pay me my wages."

Three hundred and sixty-five years on Earth. Nine months and fifteen days in space. The warp-drive had been better than ghosts had thought. Memories of McCollum and his fellows from MIT lived within the force bead, and had given it power. Better, far better, it had been, than their wildest imaginings. But Einstein had been correct. Mass, infinity, time zero. He had been correct, and Walkaway had earned three hundred and sixty-five years worth of wages. Per diem. Plus travel pay according to military regulations. They could not withhold it on grounds that he was using military transportation; Leon Packett had seen to that: Walkaway was a private citizen.

Plus interest accrued.

The sum was staggering. The sum was unbelievable. The sum could, would, *must* bankrupt the Earth government. It was unheard-of. The Prelate convened, and the arguments raged, but Walkaway needed no defense. He merely requested: "Pay me my wages." And they had to do it.

Oh, they tried to dodge their way out of it. They tried to ensnare him in legalities, but he was a man of alumasteel, and legalities could not affect him.

The circuit had closed, and his life's plan was set. In the mind of Walkaway burned the conscience and soul of his creator. Leon Packett was not dead. In his creation was re-born the intense, vibrant hatred of power and government and authority. In Walkaway was the perfect weapon; indestructible, uncaring, human as human it need be, inhuman as inhuman it *must* be, to bring about the downfall of that which Packett had despised.

Fifteen years in a cellar laboratory had carried forth for over three hundred years, and the future was molded on printed circuits.

Finally, they acceded. They paid him his wages. The government of Earth was bankrupted. The world belonged to a man of alumasteel. It was no longer Earth. Had he wished, he might have named it Walkaway's World.

For such it was.

Leon Packett had foreseen much. He had applied Einstein's equations, and he had known what would happen. The scientists of the Frericks Foundation had known, also, and they had considered it all. But the job had had to be done, in that era before Man had turned inward once more. They had feared what might happen, but not considered it an inevitability. They had looked on it the way the farmer looks on earthquake. Yes, it might happen, but that would be an act of God, not a thing that must be.

But they had not considered Leon Packett. He had taken steps. He had altered his creation, and made it want its pay, when it knew he was dead. For dead he was dead, and alive he was dead. But in the soul of Walkaway he lived again.

So he had created an act of God.

Twisted in thought, crying in the darkness of his tormented mind, Leon Packett had changed the future. Changed it so irrevocably, evened the score so beautifully, Man would remember and curse and live with his name forever. They had known of the possibility, and they had tried to prevent it.

"Let us take Walkaway back to the drawing boards," McCollum—that shadow lost in the past—had cried. But Leon Packett had overruled him, "No!"

He would not let his name and his future be stolen from him. There was no need for him to go on living out a worthless life. That was bitterness. He had a tool that would and could and needed to drive forward to his ordained destiny. He had Walkaway, and though they suspected what might be, what could be, they never thought it *needed* to be. They figured without the drive and thirst of Walkaway's master. They figured without the hatred of a man for himself and for all other men.

Walkaway wanted his wages.

He got them, by getting the Earth.

There was not that much money in the world. Nor was there that much property. But there was the government, and soon Walkaway was the government.

That was the future Leon Packett built for himself, as the shrine of his memory.

Walkaway was not vindictive.

But Leon Packett was.

There haven't been many changes. Not many. Not for us. It has been the same for a very long time.

Walkaway was fair, and carried forth Packett's desires in the only way an alumasteel man could.

Changes? No, not many.

But you'll forgive me, of course. I must hurry now. I'm quite overdue.

I should have been at my lubrication hours ago.

Man alone. Man trapped by his own nature and the limits of the world around him. Man against Man. Man against Nature. All of these inevitably come down to the essential question of how courageous a man can be in a time of massive peril. They all come down to how a man can survive, by strength of arm, by fleetness of foot, and most of all, by inventiveness of intellect. This has been the subject of much that I have written, perhaps because I see my Times and my culture in the most "hung-up" condition it has ever known. Each man, each thinking individual, for the first time in the history of the race, completely—or as near completely as prejudiced mass media will allow—aware of the forces hurling him into the future. The Bomb, ready to go whenever the finger jumps to the proper button, the ethics slowly but steadily deteriorating, the morality finding its lowest common level, and each man, each thinking individual, virtually helpless before the fluxes and flows of civilization and herd instinct. Yet, is he really alone? Ever? Or is the imagination and fierce drive to survive a tenacious linkage among us all? And if it is, then are we not brothers to the man who had

nothing for my noon meal

There was a patch of Fluhs growing out beyond the spikes, and I tried to cultivate them, and bring them around, but somehow they weren't drawing enough, and they died off before they could mature. I needed that air, too. My sac was nearly half-empty. My head was starting to hurt again. It had been night for three months at that time.

My world is a small one. Not large enough to hold an atmosphere any normal Earthman could breathe, not small enough to have none and be totally airless. My world is the sole planet of a red sun, and it has two moons, each one of which serves to eclipse my world's

146

sun for six of the eighteen months. I have light for six months, dark for twelve. I call my world Hell.

When I first came here, I had a name, and I had a face and I even had a wife. My wife died when the ship blew up, and my name died slowly over the ten years I have lived here, and my face—well, the less I remember, the easier it is for me.

Oh, I don't complain. It hasn't been easy here for me, but I've managed, and what can I say? I'm here and I'm alive as best I can be here, and what there is, there is. But what there is not, is greater than mere complaining could bring back.

The first time I saw my world was as a small egg of light in a plot tank on the ship I shared with my wife. "Do you think that has anything for us?" I asked her.

At first it was good to remember her, for when I did, a sweetness came to me, burning away my tears and my hate. At first. "I don't know, Tom, maybe." That was what she said. "Maybe." That was the sweet word, the way she said it. She always had a soft blonde way of saying *maybe* that made me want to wonder.

"The ore hold could do with something to chew on," I gibed, and she smiled with her full lips and her teeth that gently nuzzled her lower lip. "Have to pay for these damn honeymoons of yours somehow."

I kissed her playfully, for we were often happy like that; simply happy, by being together. Together. What that meant to me, I never quite knew, happy as I was. So simple was our enjoyment of one another, that it never struck me how it could be with her gone.

Then we passed through that fog of sub-atomic particles that float beyond the orbit of Firstmoon, and though they did not register on the tank, they were there and they were here and gone. Leaving in their wake a million tiny invisible holes in the hull of the ship. The holes would not have leaked enough air in a thousand years to cause my wife or myself any discomfort, but they had pierced the drive chambers, also. The particles were not rock, but something else, perhaps even contra-terrene, and what they did to the drive chambers I will never know. For the ship lost power and slewed off toward this, my world, and miles above the surface they exploded.

My wife died, then, and I saw her body as I was whirled

away in the safety section of the cab. I was safe, with great tanks of oxygen strapped to my hutch, and my wife was still there in the companionway between the metal walls. In the companionway between the galley and the cab, where she had gone to prepare me coffee.

She was still there, her arms outstretched to me, her skin quite blue—excuse me, it, it hurts still—as I was whirled away and down. I saw her that once.

My world is a harsh world. No clouds fleece its twelve-month black skies. No water runs across its surface. But then, water is no problem for me. I have the circulator, which takes my refuse, and turns it into drinkable water. There is a strong iron taste to the recirculated water, but that doesn't bother me too much.

It's the air that I have trouble getting. At least that was the case before I discovered the Fluhs had what I needed. I'll tell you about it, and about what has happened to my face; I'm frightened.

Of course I had to live.

Not at all because I wanted to live; when you have been a space bum as long as me, and nothing to moor you to one rock, and then along comes a woman who dips up life in her eyes and hands and does it all for you—and then she is taken away so quickly ...

But I had to live. Simply because I had air in the cab, and a pressure-suit and food and the circulator. I could subsist on these for quite a while.

So I lived on Hell.

I woke and went through enough hours of nothingness to make me weary, and then I slept again, and woke when my dreams grew too crimson and too loud, repeating the tracks of the "day" before. Soon I grew bored with my life in the cab, close and solitary as it was, and decided to take a walk on the surface of this world.

I slipped into my air-suit, not bothering to put on the pressure shell. There was barely enough gravity on the planet to keep me comfortable, though occasionally I got stiff pains in my chest. And with the heating circuits pressed into the material of the air-suit, I was in no real danger. I strapped the oxygen unit to my back, and slipped the bubble onto the yoke, dogging it down over my head with ease. Then I inserted the hose between oxygen unit and bubble and sealed it tightly with a wrench, so I would lose no air from leakage.

Then I went out.

It was twilight, as the sky dimmed on Hell. I had had three months of light already, since I had landed in the safety hatch, and I assumed perhaps two months of light had passed before I came. That left me with a month, roughly, before Secondmoon slipped across the face of the tiny red sun which I had not named. Even now, Secondmoon was coming across the horizon, and I knew it would be darkness for a full six months by that moon, then another six from Firstmoon, then light again for a brief six.

It had not been difficult to chart orbits and eclipse periods during the past three months. What else had I to do?

I started walking. It wasn't difficult, and I found that by taking long hops, I could cover distances three times as quickly as if I had been on Earth.

The planet was nearly barren. No great forests, no streams or oceans, no plains with grain standing in them, no birds, and no other life but mine and—

When I first saw them, I was certain they were trumpet flowers, for they had the characteristic bell-shaped perianth with delicate stamen projecting slightly from the cup. But as I drew nearer I realized nothing so Earth-like—even in outward appearance—could occur here. These were not flowers, and on the spot, in the muffled-breathing of my helmet, I called them Fluhs.

They were a brilliant orange on the outside of the bell, fading down into a bluish-orange and then a simple marine blue on the stem. Inside the cups they were not so orange as they seemed golden, and the blue of the pistils was topped by anthers of orange. Quite colorful they were, and pleasant to look upon.

There were perhaps a hundred of these plants, growing at the base of rock formations that were quite unnatural: tall and leaning at angles, and all smooth and sharp-edged, like spikes, flattened off at the tops. Not so much like rocks, but like the image of salt crystals or glass, under ultra-magnification. The entire area was covered with these formations, and with an instant's loss of reality, I seemed to see myself as a microscopic being, surrounded by great flat-edged, flat-topped crystals that were in reality merely dust or micro-specks.

Then my perspective returned, and I stepped closer to the Fluhs, to examine them more closely, for this was the only other life that had managed to exist on Hell, apparently, drawing sustenance from the thin, nitrogen-laden atmosphere.

I leaned over to stare deeper into the trumpet-blossoms, resting on one of the slanting pillars of pseudo-rock for support. That was one of my first mistakes, nearly fatal, and intended to color my entire life on Hell.

The pillar crashed—it was a semi-porous volcanic formation, almost scoria-like in composition—and loosened other rocks that had rested on it. I fell forward, directly atop the Fluhs, and the last thing I felt was my oxygen helmet shattering about my head.

Then the blackness that was not as deep as space slid down over me.

I should have been dead. There was no reason why I should not have been dead. But I was living; I was . . . breathing! Can you understand that? I should have been with my wife, but I was alive.

My face was pressed into the Fluhs.

I was drawing oxygen from them.

I had stumbled and fallen and cracked open my helmet, and should have died, but because of strange plants that sucked the nitrogen from the thin atmosphere, circulated it and cast it back out as oxygen, I was still alive. I cursed the Fluhs for depriving me of quick, unknowing surcease. I had come so close to joining her, and had lost the chance. I wanted to stagger away from the Fluhs— out into the open where they could not give me life—and gasp away my stolen life. But something stopped me. I was never a religious man, and I am not now. But there seemed to be something greater in what had happened. I can't explain it. I just *knew* there was a Chance that had thrown me down into that patch of Fluhs.

I lay there, breathing deeply.

There was a soft membrane around the base of the pistils, what must have held in the oxygen, allowing it to sift out slowly. They were intricate and wonderful plants.

. . . and there was the smell of midnight.

I can't describe it any more clearly. It was not a sweet
smell, nor was it a sour smell. It was a tender, almost
fragile odor that reminded me of one midnight when I
had first married her, and we were living in Minnesota.
Crisp, and pure and uplifting that midnight had been, when
our love had transcended even the restrictions of marriage, when we first realized we were more in love than in
love with love itself. Does that sound foolish or confused?
No, to me it was perfectly clear. And so was the smell of
midnight from the Fluhs.

It was that smell perhaps, that made me go on living.

That, and the fact that my face had begun to drain.

As I lay there, I had time to think about what this
meant: the bottleneck in oxygen lack is the brain. After
five minutes of oxygen starvation, the brain is irreversibly
damaged. But with these Fluhs, I could wander about my
planet without a helmet—were I able to find them everywhere in such abundance.

As I lay there thinking, gathering strength for the run
back to the ship, I felt my face draining. It was as
though I had a great boil or pus-bag on my left cheek, and
it was sucking blood down down into it. I felt my cheek,
and yes, even through the glove I could feel a swelling.
I grew terrified then, and plucking a handful of Fluhs—
close to the bottom of their stems—I thrust my face into
them, and ran frantically back to the ship.

Once inside, the Fluhs wilted and falling down over
my fist, they shriveled. Their brilliant colors faded, and
they turned grey as brain matter. I threw them from me
and they lay on the deckplate for a few minutes before—
they crumbled to a fine ash.

I pulled off my air-suit and my gloves, and ran to the
circulator, for it was constructed of burnished plasteel,
and my reflection lived there clearly. My left cheek was
terribly inflamed. I gave a short, sharp squeal of terror
and pawed at my face, but unlike a pimple or boil, there
was no soreness, no pain. Just the constant draining feeling.

What was there to do? I waited.

In a week, the sac had taken shape almost completely.
My face was like no human face, drawn down and puffed
out on the left side so that my left eye had been pulled into a mere slit of light shining through. It was like a gi-

gantic goiter, but a goiter that was not on the neck, but my face. The sac ended just at the jawbone, and it did not impair my breathing a bit. But my mouth had been dragged down with it, and when I opened it, I found I had a great cavernous maw instead of the firm lips I had once known. Otherwise, my face was completely normal. I was a half-beast. My right side was normal, and my left was grotesquely pulled into a drooping, rubbery satire. I could not bear to look on myself for more than an instant or two, each "day." The flaming redness of it had gone away, as had the draining, and I did not understand it for many weeks.

Until I ventured once more onto the surface of Hell.

The helmet could not be repaired, of course, so I used the one that my wife had used when she was with me. That set me thinking again, and later, when I had steadied myself, and stopped crying, I went out.

It was inevitable that I should return to the spot where my deformity had first occurred. I made the spikes, as I had now named the rock formations, without event, and sat down among a patch of Fluhs. If I had drawn off their life-giving oxygen, they seemed no worse for it, for they had continued to grow in brilliance and were, if anything, even more beautiful.

I stared at them for a long time, trying to apply what smattering of knowledge I had about the physics and chemistry of life to what had happened. It was obvious, one thing at least: I had undergone a fantastic mutation.

A mutation that was essentially impossible from what Man knew of life and its construction. What might, under exaggerated conditions, have become a permanent mutation, through generations of special breeding, had happened to me almost overnight. I tried to reason it out:

Even on a molecular scale, structure is inextricably related to function. I considered the structure of proteins, for in that direction, I felt, lay at least a partial answer to my deformity.

Finally, I removed the helmet, and bent down to the Fluhs once more. I sucked air from them, and this time felt a great light-headedness. I continued drawing, first from one flower and then the next, till I knew. My sac was full. It all became reasonably clear to me, then. The smell of midnight. There was more than just odor there. I had assimilated bacteria from the Fluhs; bacteria that had attacked the stablizing enzymes in my breathing system. Viruses perhaps, or even rickettsia, that had— for want of a clearer term—*softened* my proteins and re-shaped them to best allow me to make use of these Fluhs.

To allow me to oxygen-suck, as I had been doing, de-veloping a bigger chest or larger lungs would have done me no good. But a balloon-like organ, capable of storing oxygen under pressure . . . *that* was something else again. When I sucked from the plants, oxygen bled slowly from the blood haemoglobin into the storage sac, and after a while I would be oxygen-full.

I could then proceed without air for long periods, even as a camel can go without water for periods of great duration. Of course I would have to have an oc-casional suck to restore what I had used up in between; in an emergency, I could go without for a long while, but then I would need a *long* suck to replace completely.

How it had occurred, down in the nucleoprotein level, I was not that much of a biochemist to understand. What I knew I knew by hypno-courses I had taken many years before in the Deimos University required courses. I knew these things, but had never studied enough to be able to analyze them. Given time and sufficient references, I was sure I could unravel the mystery, for unlike Earth scien-tists, who discounted almost-instantaneous mutation as a fantasy, I *had* to believe . . . for it had happened to me. I had only to feel my face, my puffed and now ballooned face to know it was true. So I had more to work with than they did.

At that moment, I realized I had been standing erect for some minutes, my face nowhere near the Fluhs. Yet I was breathing comfortably.

Yes, I had something to work with, where they did not, for I was living the nightmare fantasy they said was im-possible.

That was six months ago. Now it is well into night, and judging from the way the Fluhs are dying, there will be nothing when light comes. Nothing left to breathe. Nothing for my noon meal.

It was so dark. The stars were too far off to care about Hell or what lived there. I should have known, of course. In the eternal darkness of twelve months' night, the Fluhs die. They don't grey-ash as the ones I first picked did. No, instead they retreat into the ground. They grow smaller and smaller, as though they were a motion picture, being run backward. They get tinier and finally disappear entirely. Whether they incyst themselves, or just die completely, I'll never know, for the ground is much too hard to dig in, and what little I've been able to scrape away, where the scoria-like formations extend into the ground, reveal nothing but small holes where the blossoms descended.

My head was starting to hurt again, and my sac was emptying out all the faster, for my breathing—which I had learned to make shallow—was deepening with the effort. I started back toward the ship.

It was many miles around the planet, for I had been living in caves and subsisting on the rations brought with me, for the past three "days." I had been trying to track down a thriving patch of Fluhs, not only to get oxygen to replenish my emptying sac, but to further study their strange metabolism. For my oxygen supply in the hutch was fast diminishing; something had gone broke in the system when I landed . . . or perhaps the same particles that had caused the ship's reactors to explode, had caused invisible damage in the oxygen recirculator. I didn't know. But I did know I had to learn to live on what Hell could give me . . . or die.

It had been a difficult decision. I had wanted very much to die.

I was standing in the open, with the heated cowl of my air-suit grotesquely drawn about my head and sac, when I saw the flickering in the deep. It burned steadily for an instant, then continued to flicker, as it fell toward the tiny planet.

I realized almost at once that it was a ship. Unbelievable, unbelievable, but somehow, in some manner I could never understand, God had sent a ship to take me from this place. I started running, back toward my hutch, what was left of my ship.

I stumbled once, and fell, only to scramble along on all fours till I could get my balance. I continued running, and by the time I had reached the hutch, my sac was nearly empty, and my head was splitting. I got inside and dogged the lock, then leaned against it in exhaustion, drawing deeply deeply for the air inside.

I turned toward the radio gear, even before the ache was gone from my head, and threw myself roughly into the plot-seat. I had almost forgotten how valuable the set could be; lost out here, so far over the Edge, I had never even given serious consideration to the possibility of being found. Actually, had I stopped to consider, it was not so peculiar after all; my ship had not exploded that far off the trade routes. True, I was far out, but any number of circumstances could combine to bring another ship my way.

And they had.

And it had.

And it was.

I flipped on the beacon signal, and set it to all-bands, hearing the bdeep-bdeep-bdeep of it in the hutch, going out, I knew, to that ship circling the planet. That done, I turned slowly in the plot chair, hands on my knees—

—only to catch sight of myself in the burnished wall of the recirculator. I saw my sac, grotesque, monstrous, hideous, covered with a week's stubble of spikey beard growth, my mouth drawn down in a gash. I was hardly human any longer.

When they came, I would not open the lock for them.

Finally, I allowed them in. There were three of them, young, clean-limbed, trying to hide their horror at what I had changed into. They came in and stripped out of their bulky pressure suits. The hatch was crowded, but the girl and one of the men squatted on the floor and the other man perched on the plot tank's edge.

"My name—" I didn't know whether to say "is" or "was" so I slurred it easily, "Tom Van Horne. I've been here about four or five months, I'm not sure which."

One of the young men—he was staring at me frankly, he could not take his eyes off me, in fact—replied, "We belong to the Human Research Foundation. Expedition to evaluate some of the worlds out past the Edge for colonization. We—we—saw the other half of your ship. There was a wom—"

I stopped him. "I know. My wife." They stared at the port, the deckplate, the bulkhead.

We talked for some time, and I could see they were interested in my theories of near-instantaneous mutation. It was their field, and soon the girl said, "Mr. Van Horne, you have stumbled on something terribly vital to us all. You *must* come back with us and help us get to the heart of—of—your, uh, your change." She blushed, and it reminded me a little of my wife.

Then the other two started in. They used me as a buffer, asking questions and answering them, and making me warmer and warmer to the prospect of returning. I was caught up in a maelstrom of enthusiasm. A feeling of belonging stole over me, and I forgot. I forgot how the ship had gone out like a match; I forgot how she had stood there frozen in the companionway, blue and strange; I forgot all the years I had spent bumming in space; I forgot the months here; and most of all I forgot the change.

They pleaded with me, and said we would go right now. I hesitated for an instant, not even knowing why, but subconsciously crying to myself to not listen. Then I relented, and got into my air-suit. When I pulled the heated cowl up about my sac, they all stared for a long moment, until the girl nudged one of the fellows, and the other broke into a nervous titter.

They jollied me, telling me how important my discovery would be to mankind. I listened; I was wanted. It was good, so good, after what had seemed an eternity on Hell.

We left my hutch, and started across the short space between their ship and my life cubicle. I was pleased and surprised to see how shining their ship was; they were proud of it, they took good care of it. They were the new breed—the high-strung, intelligent scientists with the youthful ideas and the glory in them. They weren't tired old folks like me. The ship was lighted by automatic floods that had come out on the hull, and the vessel shone in the night of Hell like a great glowing torch. It would be good aspace once more.

We came up to the ship, and one of the men depressed a stud that started a humming inside the ship. A landing ramp slid down from far above as the outer lock opened, and I knew this was a more recent model than my ship had been. But then, that didn't disturb me; I had been a poor space bum before I met her. She had been all the drive I'd ever needed.

I took a step forward, up the ramp, and two things happened, almost simultaneously:

I caught a glimpse of myself in the glowing shell of the ship. It was not a pretty picture. My ghoul's mouth, drawn down and to the side like a knife wound. My eye, a mere slit of brightness, the sac so hideous and vein-marked. I stopped on the ramp, with them directly behind me.

And the second thing happened.

I heard her.

Somewhere . . . far off . . . in a bright amber cavern hung down with scintillant stalactites . . . swathed in a shimmering aura of goodness and cleanliness and hope . . . younger than the next instant . . . radiantly beautiful and calling to me . . . calling with a voice of music that was the sound of suns flaring and stars twinkling and earth moving and grass growing and small things being happy . . . it was her!

I listened there for a moment that spanned forever.

My head tilted to the side, I listened, and I knew what she said was truth, so simple and so pure and so real, that I turned and edged past them on the ramp, and regained Hell again.

Her voice stopped in a moment of my touching ground.

They stared at me, and for a short time they said nothing. Then one of the men—the short, blonde fellow with alert blue eyes and hardly any neck—said, "What's the matter?"

"I'm not going," I said.

The girl ran down the ramp to me. "But why?" she cried.

I couldn't tell her, of course. But she was so small, so sweet, and she reminded me of my wife, when I had first met her, so I answered, "I've been here too long; I'm not very nice to look at—"

"Oh—" and she tried to stop me, but it was a sob, so it did not interfere.

"—and you may not understand this but I—I've been, well, content here. It's a hard world, and it's dark, but she's up there—" I looked toward the black sky of Hell, "—and I wouldn't want to go away and leave her alone. Can you understand that?"

They nodded slowly, and one of the men said, "But this is more than just you, Van Horne. This is a discovery that means a great deal to everyone on Earth."

"It's getting worse and worse there every year. With the new anti-agathic drugs, people just aren't dying, and they've still got the Catho-Prsybite Lobby to keep birth control laws from being enacted. The crowding is terrible; that's one of the chief reasons we're out here, to see how man can adapt to these worlds. Your discovery can aid us tremendously."

"And you said the Fluhs were gone," the other man said. "Without them, you'll die." I smiled at them; she had said something, something important about the Fluhs.

"I can still do some good," I replied quickly. "Send me a few young people. Let them come here, and we will study together. I can show them what I have found, and they can experiment here. Laboratory conditions could never match what I've found on Hell."

That seemed to do it. They looked at me sadly, and the girl agreed . . . the other two matched her agreement in a moment.

"And, and—I couldn't leave her here alone," I said again.

"Goodbye, Tom Van Horne," she said, and she pressed my hand between her mittened ones. It was a kiss on the cheek, but her helmet prevented it physically, so she clasped my hand.

Then they started up the ramp.

"What will you do for air, with the Fluhs gone?" one of the men asked, stopping halfway up.

"I'll be all right, I promise you. I'll be here when you return." They looked at me with doubt, but I smiled, and patted my sac, and they looked uncomfortable, and started up the ramp again.

"We'll be back. With others." The girl looked down at me. I waved, and they went inside. Then I loped back to the hutch, and watched them as they shattered the night with their fire and fury. When they were gone, I went outside, and stared up at the dim, so-faraway points of the dead stars.

Where she circled, up there, somewhere.

And I knew I would have something for my noon meal, and all the meals thereafter. She had told me; I suppose I knew it all along, but it hadn't registered, but she had told me: the Fluhs were not dead. They had merely gone down to replenish their own oxygen supply from the planet itself, from the caves and porous openings where the rock trapped the air. They would be back again, long before I needed them.

The Fluhs would return.

And some day I would find her again, and it would be an unbroken time.

This world I had named, I had named not properly. Not Hell.

Not Hell at all.

There really isn't much to say about this next story, save that I've tried to make a bit of a caustic comment on the "faithful" and their faith. I have no quarrel with those who wish to believe—whether they believe in a flat Earth, the health-giving properties of sorghum and blackstrap molasses, Dianetics, the Hereafter, orgone boxes, a ghost-writer for Shakespeare, or that jazz about the manna in the desert—except to point out that nothing in this life (and presumably the next) is certain; and faith is all well and good, but even the most devout should leave a small area of their thoughts open for such possibilities as occur in

hadj

It had taken almost a year to elect Herber. A year of wild speculation, and a growing sense of the Universe's existence. The year after the Masters of the Universe had flashed through Earth's atmosphere and broadcast their message.

From nowhere they had come down in their glowing golden spaceship—forty miles long—and without resistance shown every man, woman, and child on Earth that they did, indeed, rule the Universe.

They had merely said: "Send us a representative from Earth." They had then given detailed instructions for constructing what they called an "inverspace" ship, and directions for getting to their home world, somewhere across the light-galaxies.

So the ship had been constructed. But who was to go? The Earthmen who pondered this question knew the awesome responsibility of that emissary. They had to be careful whom they picked. So they had reasoned it was too big a problem to lay in the hands of mere humans, and set the machines on it. They had set the Mark XXX, the UniCompVac, the Brognagov Master Computer and hundreds of the little brains to the task.

After sixteen billion punched cards had gone through three times, the last card fell into the hopper, and Wilson

Herber had been elected. *He* was the most fit to travel across the hundred galaxies to the home world of the Masters of the Universe, and offer his credentials to them.

They came to Wilson Herber in his mountain retreat, and were initially greeted by threats of disembowelment if they didn't get the hell away and leave him in his retirement!

But judicious reasoning soon brought the ex-statesman around. Herber was one of the wealthiest men in the world. The cartel he had set up during the first fifty-six years of his life was still intact, run entirely now by his lieutenants. It spanned every utility and service, every raw material and necessity a growing Earth would need. It had made Wilson Herber an incalculably wealthy man. It had led him into the World Federation Hall, where he had served as Representative for ten years, till he had become Co-Ordinator of the Federation.

Then, five years before the golden Masters had come, he had completely retired, completely secluded himself. Only a matter of such import could bring the crusty, hard-headed old pirate out of his sanctuary—and throw him into the stars.

"I'll take the credentials," he advised the men who had come to him. He sat sunk deep in an easy chair, a shrunken gnome of a man with thinned grey hair, piercing blue eyes, and a chin sharp as a diamond facet.

"You must establish us on a sound footing with their emissaries, and let them know we walk hand-in-hand with them, as brothers," one of the men had told Herber.

"Till we can get what we might need from them, and then assume their position ourselves, young man?" Herber had struck directly—and embarrassingly—to the heart of the question.

The young man had hummed and hawed, and finally smiled down grimly at the old ex-statesman. "You always know best, Sir."

And Wilson Herber had smiled. Grimly.

The planet rose out of Inverspace. It was incredible, but they had somehow devised a way to insert their world through the fabric of space itself, and let it impinge into not-space.

Herber, cushioned in a special travel-chair, sat beside

Captain Arnand Singh, watching the half-circle that was their planet-in-Inverspace wheeling beneath the ship.

"Impressive, wouldn't you say, Captain?"

The Moslem nodded silently. He was a huge man, giving the impression of compactness and efficiency. "This is almost like a hadj, Mr. Herber," he noted.

Wilson Herber drew his eyes away from the ship-circling viewslash and stared at the brown-skinned officer. "Eh? Hadj? What's that?"

"What my people once called a pilgrimage to Mecca. Here are we, Earthmen, journeying to this other Mecca..."

Herber cut him off. "Listen, boy. Just remember this: we're as good as them any day, and they know it. Otherwise they wouldn't have extended us any invitation. We're here to establish diplomatic relations, as with any foreign power. So get this Hadj business out of you."

The Moslem did not answer, but a faint smile quirked his lips at the bravado of the man. The first Earthmen to visit the Masters' home-world, and he was treating it as though it were a trip to a foreign embassy in New New York. He liked the old man, though he had a healthy dislike for the inherent policies he stood for.

All that was cut off in his mind as the control board bleeped for slip-out. "Better fasten those pads around you, sir," he advised, helping lay the protective coverings about the old man's body, "we're just about ready to translate."

Herber's wonderously-outfitted diplomatic ship settled down through the shifting colors of Inverspace, and abruptly translated out.

In normal space, the planet was even more imposing.

Forty-mile-high buildings of delicate pastel tracery reached for the sky. Huge ships plied back and forth in a matter of minutes, between the three large continents.

There were unrecognizable constructions everywhere: evidence of a highly advanced science, a complicated culture. There was evidence everywhere of the superior intellect of these people. Herber sat beside the Captain and smiled.

"We can learn a great deal from these people, Singh," he said quietly, almost reverently. His pinched, wrinkled features settled into an expression of momentary rest.

This was an ultimate end. They had found their brothers in the stars.

"Now to offer our credentials. Hand me the beamer, will you, Singh. Ah . . . that's good . . . thanks. I hope they get the escort ships out quickly . . . I can't wait to see that world close up. Why, the secret of their instantaneous shipping—see how those ships disappear, and reappear over there!—that's enough to ruin my cartel! Wonderful stuff they have down there . . . can't wait to . . . well, that'll all come later."

He raised the beamer to his lips, and the transmitter arced the message out:

"We are the emissaries from Earth, here to offer you the fellowship and knowledge of our planet. We hope our brothers of the golden world are well. We request landing instructions."

They waited. Singh spotted the spaceport, a huge and sprawling eighty-mile-wide affair with gigantic loading docks and golden ships aimed at the skies. He settled toward it, waiting for the signal to land.

Finally, the sound came back:

"Owoooo, oowah wawooooo eeeeyahh, wooooo . . ."

Herber's shriveled gnome face split into anger. "Translate it, Captain! Dammit, man, translate! We can't take a chance on missing a note of introduction in any particular!"

The Captain hurriedly turned on the translator, and the sounds were re-routed. In a moment they came through, repeating the same message over and over, to the brothers from Earth. Wilson Herber listened, and his wrinkled face was overcome by an expression even *he* could not name.

After a while they didn't bother listening. They just sat in the cab of the diplomatic ship, staring out at the golden world, these brothers from space, and the words echoed hollowly in their ears:

"Please go around to the service entrance. Please go around to the service entrance. Please . . ."

When I first arrived in New York, the city was in the midst of its Monsoon Season: January to December. After mooching room, board and writing counsel from Lester del Rey and his wife Evelyn for a few days, I moved into one of the great abodes of memorabilia in my life—a hotel on West 114th Street, where already resided Robert Silverberg, the writer, who had been attending Columbia University and selling stories on the side (or vice versa). In the first week of my residence, I completed three short stories. The first was sold to Larry Shaw, then editor of Infinity, and provided rent for several weeks to come. The second sold to Guilty Detective Story Magazine, and provided food for the tummy. The third was prompted by the dreadful weather, the silver rain that fell past my third floor window hour after hour. It did not sell till three years later, to the British magazine Science Fantasy. *I rather liked the yarn, and could never understand why American science-fiction magazines were not devious enough to slip in a little straight fantasy every now and then. But since they don't, I'm pleased to be able to have that third-written story in print again in this country, reminding me of my days of childhood naturalism in New York, when I stood before my grimy window and rather hysterically murmured*

rain, rain, go away

Sometimes I wish I were a duck, mused Hobert Krouse. Standing in front of his desk, looking out the window at the amount of water the black sky had begun to let flow, his thoughts rolled in the same trough made for them years before.

"Rain, rain, go away, come again another . . ." he began, *sotto voce*.

"*Krouse!* Come away from that window and get back to those weather analyses, man, or you'll be out *walking* in that, instead of just looking at it!" The voice had a sandpaper edge, and it rasped across Hobert's senses in much the same way real sandpaper might. Hobert gasped

164

involuntarily and turned. Mr. Beigen stood, florid and annoyed, framed in the big walnut timbers of the entrance to his office.

"I—I was just looking at the rain, sir. You see, my predictions *were* correct. It *is* going to be a prolonged wet spell . . ." Hobert began, obsequiously sliding back into his swivel chair.

"*Balderdash,* man," Mr. Beigen roared, "nothing of the sort! I've told you time and again, Krouse, leave the predictions to the men who are paid for that sort of thing. You just tend to your checking, and leave the brainwork to men who have the equipment. Prolonged rain, indeed! All my reports say fair.

"And let's have that be the *last* time we see you at something other than your job during work hours, Krouse. Which are eight-thirty to five, six days a week," he added.

With a quick glance across the rest of the office, immobilizing every person there with its rockiness, Beigen went back into his office, the door slamming shut with finality.

Hobert thought he caught a fragment of a sentence, just as the door banged closed. It sounded like, "Idiot," but he couldn't be sure.

Hobert did not like the tone Mr. Beigen had used in saying it was the *last time* he wanted to see him away from his desk. It sounded more like a promise than a demand.

The steady pound of the rain on the window behind him made him purse his lips in annoyance. Even though his job was only checking the weather predictions sent down from the offices upstairs against the messages sent out by the teletype girls, still he had been around the offices of Havelock, Beigen and Elsesser long enough to take a crack at predicting himself.

Even though Mr. Beigen was the biggest man in the wholesale farm supply business, and Hobert was one small link in a chain employing many hundreds of people, still he didn't have to scream that way, did he? Hobert worried for a full three minutes, until he realized that the stack of invoices had been augmented by yet another pile from the Gloversville, Los Angeles and Topeka teletypes. He began furiously trying to catch up. Something which he would never quite be able to do.

Walking home in the rain, his collar turned up, his bowler pulled down tight over his ears, the tips of his shoes beginning to lose their shine from the water, Hobert's thoughts began to take on a consistency much like the angry sky above him.

Eight years in the offices of Havelock, Beigen and Elsesser had done nothing for him but put sixty-eight dollars and fifty-five cents into his hand each week. The work was an idiot's chore, and though Hobert had never finished college, still it was a job far beneath his capabilities.

Hobert's section of the firm was one of those little services rendered to farmers within the reach of the company's services. A long-range weather forecast for all parts of the country, sent free each week to thousands of subscribers.

A crack of thunder split Hobert's musings, forcing him to a further awareness of the foul weather. Rain had soaked him from hat crown to shoe soles and even gotten in through his upturned collar, to run down his back in chilly threads. He began to wish there might be someone waiting home for him with the newspaper (the one he had bought at the corner was now a sodden mass) and his slippers, but he knew there would not be.

Hobert had never married—he had just not found *the* girl he told himself must come to him. In fact, the last affair he could recall having had was five years before, when he had gone up to Bear Mountain for two weeks. She had been a Western Union telegraph operator named Alice, with very silky chestnut hair, and for a while Hobert had thought perhaps. But he had gone back to New York and she had gone back to Trenton, New Jersey, without even a formal goodbye, and Hobert despaired of ever finding The One.

He walked down West 52nd to Seventh Avenue, scuffing his feet in irritation at the puddles which placed themselves so he could not fail to walk through them, soaking his socks. At 50th he boarded the subway uptown and all the way sat brooding.

Who does Beigen think he is, Hobert seethed within himself. I've been in that office eight years, three months and . . . well, I've been there well over eight years, three months. Who does he think he's pushing around like

that? I may be a little smaller, but I'll be (his mind forti-
fied itself) *damned* (his mind looked around in embar-
rassment to see if anyone had noticed) if I'll take treat-
ment like that. I'll—I'll *quit*, that's what I'll do. I'll quit.
Then where will he be? Who'll he get to fill my job as
capably as I can?

But even as he said it, he could see the ad in the
Herald-Tribune the night he would resign:

OFFICE Boy-clk, 18-20 exc. future $40 no exp. nec.
Havelock, Beigen & Elsesser 229 W 52.

He could see it so clearly in his mind because that had
been the ad to which he had replied, eight years, three
months and an undetermined number of weeks before.

The mindless roar of the train hurtling through the
subway dimmed for Hobert and, as happens to everyone
occasionally, everything summed up for him. The eight
years summed up. His life summed up.

"I'm a failure." He said it aloud, and heads turned toward him, but he didn't notice. He said it again in his
mind, clearer this time, for it was true and he knew it:
I'm a failure.

I've never been to Puerto Rico or India or even to
Trenton, New Jersey, he thought. The furthest away from
this city I've been is Bear Mountain, and that was only
for two weeks. I've never really loved anyone—except
Mother, he hastened to add; and she's been gone thirteen
years now—and no one has ever really loved me.

When the line of thoughts had run itself out, Hobert
looked up, misty-eyed, and saw that he had gone past his
station. He got off, walked over and took the downtown
train back to West 110th.

In his room, cramped by books and periodicals so that
free space was nearly non-existent, Hobert removed his
wet hat and coat, hung them near the radiator, and sat
down on the bed, which served as a couch. I wish something truly unusual would happen to me, thought Hobert.
I wish something so spectacular would happen that everyone would turn as I went down the street, and say, "There
goes Hobert Krouse; what a *man!*" And they would have
awe and wonder in their eyes. I wish it would happen to
me just once. "Every man is entitled to fame at least once
in his lifetime!" He said it with force, for he believed it.

But nothing happened, and Hobert went to bed that night with the wind howling through the space between the apartment buildings and with the rain beating against his window.

Perhaps it will wash some of that dirt off the outside, he mused, thinking of the window that had not been clean since he had moved in. But then, it was five floors up and the custodian wouldn't hire a window-washer and it was too dangerous out there for Hobert to do it. Sleep began to press down on him, the sure feel of it washing away his worries of the day. Almost as an incantation he repeated the phrase he had remembered from his childhood, the phrase he had murmured thousands of times since. "Rain, rain, go away, come again another day." He began the phrase again, but sleep cut it off in mid-thought.

It rained all that week, and by Sunday morning, when Hobert emerged from the brownstone face of his building, the ground around the one lone tree growing slantwise on the sloping 110th sidewalk was mushy and runny. The gutters were swollen with flowing torrents. Hobert looked up at the darkened sky which was angry even at eleven in the morning, with no trace of sun.

In annoyance he ran through the "Rain, rain, go away," nonsense and trudged up the hill to the corner of Broadway for breakfast.

In the little restaurant, his spread-bottom drooping over a stool too small for his pear shape, Hobert gave huge traditional leers to Florence, the redhead behind the counter, and ordered the usual: "Two up, ham steak, coffee, cream, Florence."

As he ate his eggs, Hobert returned again to his wistful dreams of a few evenings previous.

"Florence," he said, "you ever wish something spectacular would happen to you?" He pushed a mouthful of toast and ham around his tongue to get the sentence out.

Florence looked up from her duty; putting rock-hard butter squares on paper pads. "Yeah, I useta wish somethin'd happen ta me," she pushed a string of red hair back into place, "but it never did." She shrugged.

"Like what did you wish?" inquired Hobert.

"Oh, *you* know. Silly stuff, like whyn't Mahlon Brando come in here an' grab me an' like that. Or whyn't I win a millyun bucks in the Irish Sweepstakes and come back here some aftuhnoon wearin' a mink stole and flip the end of it in that stinkin' Erma Geller's kisser. *You* know." She went back to the butter.

Hobert knew. He had made equivalent wishes himself, with particulars slightly changed. It had been Gina Lollobrigida and a $250 silk shantung suit like Mr. Beigen owned, when *he* had daydreams.

He finished the eggs and ham, wiped up the last little drippings of egg yellow, bolted his coffee, and, wiping his mouth with his paper napkin, said, "Well, see you tomorrow, Florence."

She accepted the exact change he left for the bill, noted the usual fifteen cents under the plate and said, "Ain'tcha comin' in for dinner tonight?"

Hobert assumed an air of bored detachment, "No, no, I think I shall go downtown and take in a show tonight. Or perhaps I shall dine at The Latin Quarter or Lindy's. With pheasant under glass and caviar and some of that famous Lindy's cheesecake. I shall decide when I get down there." He began to walk out, joviality in his walk.

"Oh, ya *such* a character," laughed Florence, behind him.

But the rain continued, and Hobert only went a few streets down Broadway where the storm had driven everyone off the sidewalks, with the exception of those getting the Sunday editions. "Lousy day," he muttered under his breath. Been like this all week, he observed to himself. That ought to teach that bigmouth Beigen that maybe I can predict as well as his high-priced boys upstairs. Maybe *now* he'll listen to me!

Hobert could see Mr. Beigen coming over to his desk, stammering for a moment, then, putting his arm around Hobert's shoulders—which Hobert carefully ignored—telling Hobert he was terribly sorry and he would never scream again, and would Hobert forgive him for his rudeness and here was a fifteen dollar raise and a job upstairs in the analysis department.

Hobert could see it all. Then the wetness of his socks, clinging to his ankles, made the vision fade. Oh, rain, rain!

The movie was just opening, and though Hobert despised Barbara Stanwyck, he went in to kill the time. It was lonely for a pot-bellied man of forty-six in New York without any close friends and all the current books and magazines read.

Hobert tsk-tsked all the way through the picture, annoyed at the simpleton plot. He kept thinking to himself that if he had one wish he would wish she never made another picture.

When he emerged, three hours later, it was afternoon and the rain whipped into the alcove behind the ticket booth drenching him even before he could get onto the street. It was a cold rain, wetter than any Hobert could remember, and thick, with no space between drops, it seemed. As though God were tossing down all the rain in the heavens at once.

Hobert began walking, humming to himself the little rain, rain ditty. His mind began trying to remember how many times he had uttered that series of words. He failed, for it stretched back to his childhood. Every time he had seen a rainfall he had made the same appeal. And he was surprised to realize now that it had worked almost uncannily, many times.

He could recall one sunny day when he was twelve, that his family had set aside for a picnic. It had suddenly darkened and begun to come down scant minutes before they were to leave.

Hobert remembered having pressed himself up flat against the front room windows, one after another, wildly repeating the phrase over and over. The windows had been cold, and his nose had felt funny, all flattened up that way. But after a few minutes it had worked. The rain had stopped, the sky had miraculously cleared, and they went to Huntington Woods for the picnic. It hadn't been a really good picnic, but that wasn't important. What *was* important was that *he* had stopped the rain with his own voice.

For many years thereafter Hobert had believed that. And he had applied the rain, rain ditty as often as he could, which was quite often. Sometimes it never seemed to work, and others it did. But whenever he got around to saying it, the rain never lasted too long afterward.

Wishes, wishes, wishes, ruminated Hobert. If I had one wish, what would I wish? Would the wish really come true?

Or do you have to keep repeating your wish? Is that the secret? Is that why some people get what they want eventually, because they make the same wish, over and over, the same way till it comes true? Perhaps we all have the ability to make our wishes come true, but we must persist in them, for belief and the strength of your convictions is a powerful thing. If I had one wish, what would I wish? I'd wish that . . .

It was then, just as Hobert saw the Hudson River beginning to overflow onto Riverside Drive, rising up and up over the little park along the road, that he realized.

"Oh my goodness!" cried Hobert, starting up the hill as fast as he could.

"Rain, rain, go away, come again another day."

Hobert said it, sprayed his throat, and made one more chalk mark on the big board full of marks. He said it again, and once more marked.

It was odd. All that rain *had* gone away, only to come another day. The unfortunate part was that it *all* came back the same day. Hobert was—literally speaking—up the creek. He had been saying it since he was a child, how many times he had no idea. The postponements had been piling up for almost forty-six years, which was quite a spell of postponements. The only way he could now stop the flood of rain was to keep saying it, and say it one more time than all the times he had said it during those forty-six years. And the next time all forty-six years plus the one before plus another. And so on. And so on.

The water was lapping up around the cornice of his building, and Hobert crouched further into his rubber raft on its roof, pulling the big blackboard toward him, repeating the phrase, chalking, spraying occasionally.

It wasn't bad enough that he was forced to sit there repeating, repeating, repeating all day, just to stop the rain, there was another worry nagging Hobert's mind.

Though it had stopped raining now, for a while, and though he was fairly safe on the roof of his building, Hobert was worried. For when the weather became damp, he invariably caught laryngitis.

Friendship, that most fleeting of human relationships, seems to me to be one of the most precious. The old saw about "he is a rich man who can truly say he has three true friends" may be saccharine, but it has its merits. The vagaries of the human spirit, particularly in times as debilitating and sorrowful as these, seem almost to stack the deck against lasting friendships. And I wonder how much more valuable and difficult they will be, in our particular future, when man has been consigned to numerous oases in the sea of stars. I think many will find their prejudices and fears being swept away in the face of their needs for companionship, particularly

in lonely lands

"He clasps the crag with crooked hands;
"Close to the sun in lonely lands,
"Ring'd with the azure world he stands."
ALFRED, LORD TENNYSON

Pederson knew night was falling over Syrtis Major; blind, still he knew the Martian night had arrived; the harp crickets had come out. The halo of sun's warmth that had kept him golden through the long day had dissipated, and he could feel the chill of the darkness now. Despite his blindness there was an appreciable *changing* in the shadows that lived where once, long ago, there had been sight.

"Pretrie," he called into the hush, and the answering echoes from the moon valleys answered and answered, *Pretrie, Pretrie, Pretrie,* down and down, almost to the foot of the small mountain.

"I'm here, Pederson old man. What do you want of me?"

Pederson relaxed in the pneumorack. He had been tense for some time, waiting. Now he relaxed. "Have you been to the temple?"

"I was there. I prayed for many turnings, through three colors."

173

It had been many years since Pederson had seen colors. But he knew the Martian's religion was strong and stable because of colors. "And what did the blessed Jilka fore-tell, Pretrie?"

"Tomorrow will be cupped in the memory of today. And other things." The silken overtones of the alien's voice were soothing. Though Pederson had never seen the tall, utterly ancient Jilkite, he had passed his arthritic, spatulate fingers over the alien's hairless, teardrop head, had seen by feeling the deep round sockets where eyes glowed, the pug nose, the thin, lipless gash that was mouth. Pederson knew this face as he knew his own, with its wrinkles and sags and protuberances. He knew the Jilkite was so old no man could estimate it in Earth years.

"Do you hear the Grey Man coming yet?"

Pretrie sighed, a lung-deep sigh, and Pederson could hear the inevitable crackling of bones as the alien hunkered down beside the old man's pneumorack.

"He comes but slowly, old man. But he comes. Have patience."

"Patience," Pederson chuckled ruminatively. "I got that, Pretrie. I got that and that's about all. I used to have time, too, but now that's about gone. You say he's coming?"

"Coming, old man. Time. Just time."

"How are the blue shadows, Pretrie?"

"Thick as fur in the moon valleys, old man. Night is coming."

"Are the moons out?"

There was a breathing through wide nostrils—ritualistically slit nostrils—and the alien replied, "None yet this night. Tayseff and Teei are below the horizon. It grows dark swiftly. Perhaps this night old man."

"Perhaps," Pederson agreed.

"Have patience."

Pederson had not always had patience. As a young man, the blood warm in him, he had fought with his Presby-Baptist father, and taken to space. He had not believed in Heaven, Hell, and the accompanying rigors of the All-Church. Not then. Later, but not then.

To space he had gone, and the years had been good to him. He had aged slowly, healthily, as men do in the dark places between dirt. Yet he had seen the death, and the men who had died believing, the men who had died not believing. And with time had come the realization that he was alone, and that some day, one day, the Grey Man would come for him.

He was always alone, and in his loneliness, when the time came that he could no longer tool the great ships through the star-spaces, he went away.

He went away, searching for a home, and finally came full-circle to the first world he had known; came home to Mars, where he had been young, where his dreams had been born; Mars, for home is always where a man has been young and happy. Came home where the days were warm and the nights were mild. Came home where men had passed but somehow, miraculously, had not sunk their steel and concrete roots. Came home to a home that had changed not at all since he'd been young. And it was time. For blindness had found him, and the slowness that forewarned him of the Grey Man's visit. Blindness from too many glasses of vik and scotch, from too much hard radiation, from too many years of squinting into the vastnesses. Blind, and unable to earn his keep.

So alone, he had come home; as the bird finds the tree, as the winter-starved deer finds the last bit of bark, as the water quenches the thirst. He had come there to wait for the Grey Man, and it was there that the Jilkite Pretrie had found him.

They sat together, silently, on the porch with many things unsaid, yet passing between them.

"Pretrie?"

"Old man."

"I never asked you what you get out of this. I mean—"

Pretrie reached and the sound of his claw tapping the formica table-top came to Pederson. Then the alien was pressing a bulb of water-diluted vik into his hand. "I know what you mean, old man. I have been with you close on two harvestings. I am here. Does that not satisfy you?"

Two harvestings. Equivalent to four years Earth-time, Pederson knew. The Jilkite had come out of the dawn one day, and stayed to serve the old blind man. Pederson had never questioned it. One day he was struggling with the coffee pot (he dearly loved old-fashion brewed coffee and scorned the use of the coffee briquettes) and the heat controls on the hutch . . . the next he had an undemanding, unselfish manservant who catered with dignity and regard to his every desire. It had been a companionable relationship; he had made no great demands on Pretrie, and the alien had asked nothing in return.

He was in no position to wonder or question.

Though he could hear Pretrie's brothers in the chesthigh floss brakes at harvesting time, still the Jilkite never wandered far from the hutch.

Now, it was nearing its end.

"It has been easier with you here. I—uh—thanks, Pretrie," the old man felt the need to say it clearly, without embroidery.

A soft grunt of acknowledgment. "I thank you for allowing me to remain with you, old man, Pederson," the Jilkite answered softly.

A spot of cool touched Pederson's cheek. At first he thought it was rain, but no more came, and he asked, "What was that?"

The Jilkite shifted—with what Pederson took for discomfort—and answered, "A custom of my race."

"What?" Pederson persisted.

"A tear, old man. A tear from my eye to your body."

"Hey, look . . ." he began, trying to convey his feelings, and realizing *look* was the wrong word. He stumbled on, an emotion coming to him he had long thought dead inside himself. "You don't have to be—uh—you know, sad, Pretrie. I've lived a good life. The Grey Man doesn't scare me." His voice was brave, but it cracked with the age in the cords.

"My race does not know sadness, Pederson. We know gratitude and companionship and beauty. But not sadness. That is a serious lack, so you have told me, but we do not yearn after the dark and the lost. My tear is a thank you for your kindness."

"Kindness?"

"For allowing me to remain with you."

The old man subsided then, waiting. He did not understand. But the alien had found him, and the presence of

Pretrie had made things easier for him in these last years. He was grateful, and wise enough to remain silent.

They sat there thinking their own thoughts, and Pederson's mind winnowed the wheat of incidents from the chaff of life spent.

He recalled the days alone in the great ships, and how he had at first laughed to think of his father's religion, his father's words about loneliness: "No man walk the road without companionship, Will," his father had said. He had laughed, declaring he was a loner, but now, with the unnameable warmth and presence of the alien here beside him, he knew the truth.

His father had been correct.

It was good to have a friend. Especially when the Grey Man was coming. Strange how he knew it with such calm certainty, but that was the way of it. He knew, and he waited placidly.

After a while, the chill came down off the hills, and Pretrie brought out the treated shawl. He laid it about the old man's thin shoulders, where it clung with warmth, and hunkered down on his triple-jointed legs once more.

"I don't know, Pretrie," Pederson ruminated, later.

There was no answer. There had been no question.

"I just don't know. Was it worth it all? The time aspace, the men I've known, the lonely ones who died and the dying ones who were never lonely."

"All peoples know that ache, old man," Pretrie philosophized. He drew a deep breath.

"I never thought I needed anyone. I've learned better, Pretrie."

"One never knows." Pederson had taught the alien little; Pretrie had come to him speaking English. It had been one more puzzling thing about the Jilkite, but again Pederson had not questioned it. There had been many spacers and missionaries on Mars.

"Everybody needs somebody," Pederson went on.

"You will never know," Pretrie agreed, then added, "perhaps you will."

Then the alien stiffened, his claw upon the old man's arm. "He comes, Pederson old man."

A thrill of expectancy, and a shiver of near-fright came with it. Pederson's grey head lifted, and despite the warmth of the shawl he felt cold. So near now. "He's coming?"

"He is here."

They both sensed it, for Pederson could feel the awareness in the Jilkite beside him; he had grown sensitive to the alien's moods, even as the other had plumbed his own. "The Grey Man," Pederson spoke the words softly on the night air, and the moon valleys did not respond.

"I'm ready," said the old man, and he extended his left hand for the grasp. He set down the bulb of vik with his other hand.

The feel of hardening came stealing through him, and it was as though someone had taken his hand in return. Then, as he thought he was to go, alone, he said, "Goodbye to you, Pretrie, friend."

But there was no good-bye from the alien beside him. Instead, the Jilkite's voice came to him as through a fog softly descending.

"We go together, friend Pederson. The Grey Man comes to all races. Why do you expect me to go alone? Each need is a great one.

"I am here, Grey Man. Here. I am not alone." Oddly, Pederson knew the Jilkite's claw had been offered, and taken in the clasp.

He closed his blind eyes.

After a great while, the sound of the harp crickets thrummed high once more, and on the porch before the hutch, there was the silence of peace.

Night had come to the lonely lands; night, but not darkness.

More SIGNET Science Fiction Books You'll Enjoy

☐ **MOON OF MUTINY by Lester del Rey.** Set in the early days of the moon's colonization, this exciting novel tells of one man's escapades in a new frontier.

(#Q5539—95¢)

☐ **ELEMENT 79 by Fred Hoyle.** A noted astronomer and science fiction author leads an excursion into a fantastic —but scientifically possible—future universe in this engaging collection of stories. (#Q5279—95¢)

☐ **THE BLACK CLOUD by Fred Hoyle.** Earth was menaced by a power from beyond the stars and older than time.

(#T5486—75¢)

☐ **GARDEN ON THE MOON by Pierre Boulle.** In a rousing science fiction tale, the renowned author of **Planet of the Apes** captures the tension of the race to put man on the moon. (#Q5806—95¢)

☐ **THE PEOPLE OF THE WIND by Poul Anderson.** Avalon, planet of Ythri and Terran alike, was caught in the center of a galactic power struggle. Claimed by both sides, Avalon had only her secret weapon to protect her against the combined might of the two empires. Could one small planet survive while empires crumbled?

(#Q5479—95¢)

☐ **THE MAN WHO SOLD THE MOON by Robert A. Heinlein.** The daring adventures of the bold men of tomorrow told as only the master of science fiction can.

(#Y6233—$1.25)

SIGNET Science Fiction You Will Enjoy

Other SIGNET Science Fiction Titles You Will Enjoy